The Solitary Twin

Other Books by Harry Mathews

FICTION

The Conversions • Tlooth • Country Cooking and Other Stories
The Sinking of the Odradek Stadium • Cigarettes
Singular Pleasures • The American Experience • The Journalist
Sainte Catherine • The Human Country: New and Collected Stories
My Life in CIA

POETRY

The Ring: Poems 1956–1969 • The Planisphere • Trial Impressions
Le Savoir des rois • Armenian Papers: Poems 1954–1984
Out of Bounds • A Mid-Season Sky: Poems 1954–1991
Alphabet Gourmand (with Paul Fournel) • The New Tourism

MISCELLANIES

Selected Declarations of Dependence • The Way Home
Écrits Français

NONFICTION & CRITICISM

The Orchard: A Remembrance of Georges Perec • 20 Lines a Day
Immeasurable Distances • Giandomenico Tiepolo
Oulipo Compendium (with Alastair Brotchie)
The Case of the Persevering Maltese: Collected Essays

Harry Mathews

THE SOLITARY TWIN

A novel

A NEW DIRECTIONS BOOK

Manufactured in the United States of America
New Directions Books are printed on acid-free paper
First published as a New Directions Paperbook (NDP1402) in 2018

Library of Congress Cataloging-in-Publication Data
Names: Mathews, Harry, 1930–2017, author.
Title: The solitary twin / Harry Mathews.
Description: New York : New Directions Publishing, [2018]
Identifiers: LCCN 2017041783 (print) | LCCN 2017045132 (ebook) |
ISBN 9780811227551 | ISBN 9780811227544 (softcover : acid-free paper)
Subjects: LCSH: Interpersonal relations—Fiction. |
City and town life—Fiction. | Twins—Fiction.
Classification: LCC PS3563.A8359 (ebook) | LCC PS3563.A8359 S67 2018 (print) |
DDC 813/.54—dc23
LC record available at https://lccn.loc.gov/2017041783

2 4 6 8 10 9 7 5 3 1

New Directions Books are published for James Laughlin
by New Directions Publishing Corporation
80 Eighth Avenue, New York 10011

for Ann Beattie

1

Berenice Tinker says, "When wine is to your taste, it has a becoming effect on you. You shine through your reticence," to which Andreas Boeyens replies, "You're modest, darling. It isn't the wine." "Thank you for your recent attentions; but I'm talking about something real, like a measurable physical effect." "See what I mean?" "Please, no slick flick dialogue. Do you not drink sourpuss martinis to 'mortify a taste for vintages'?" "Then no quality-lite bites either." "If you insist."

Later that evening, Berenice: "I garbled my thought. I told you I met John today. He lectured me sweetly about feelings for so long I lost touch with what the word means, at least until you unforeseeably slid into my bed. Actually not so unforeseeably, I've since realized." "The hots at first sight?" "Happily so. However, I once saw a picture of you with your sister in a gossip mag. We are decidedly the same type." "You are nothing like my sister. You are absorbingly new to me." "Maybe. A feeling, perhaps?" "And have you seen my anticipatory sibling?" "I wondered. No brother. But your hair is the color of the gigantic poodle that belonged to Uncle Dom. When I was still an infant, it used to make me weep tears of terror whenever we visited him. As you approached, your lovely ginger hair filled me with darkest emotion. That must do for the time being." "Charming! Sweet John, really! Just what else did he say to you?"

Berenice and Andreas, too foolish to sense the truth, were blessed with something of utmost price: a happiness beyond what either of them had ever imagined. They were sitting in Berenice's house above the town. A strange town. For years it had survived as an extenuated fishing village of immemorial origin. Then, in the 1870s, it had started building itself deliberately (if inexplicably) into a settlement many times its size, in accordance (no less inexplicably) with a layout evoking the frugal plans of medieval towns more than the optimistic spreads of the late nineteenth century. Houses, shops, an inn, a market place, two churches, two bars, and a few public eateries were bonded together in a cluster occupying less than seventeen acres. Around the top of this area ran a road that proved as solid a barrier as any town wall of old: there was never any question of expanding beyond it, fair as the land there became, and free of danger. The coast of the bay mainly displayed jagged outcroppings of laminated schist; inland rose hills of soft-green vegetation punctuated occasionally with stands of beech, maple, and feathery conifers. A few hundred yards from the town one came upon large houses, often faced with yellow brick and fitted with multiple windows, whose purpose, one guessed, was to allow their occupants to feast their eyes on the green space around them, a prospect that even the best-appointed houses of the mother-town could never provide. It was one of these pleasant dwellings that Berenice had rented two days after her arrival.

Berenice: "You must realize that my hypothesis reflects a professional weakness, a penchant for cracking open every nut for study. This was only the first squeeze of the nut cracker. The next one may reveal, if not a chief jewel, at least something more acceptable to you. John said nothing to suggest the hair of the dog. He wanted to persuade me that feelings are our only reality ..." "How delicious!" "... our only currency. Speaking our feelings and not what we think we ought to say is our only way of speaking truthfully. He quoted some poet (I'm not breaking my promise, just reporting *his* words), 'And I see in flashes / what you already said, / that our feelings are our facts'." Andreas groaned. Berenice: "What's the harm in that? John hasn't an ounce of malice in him." "Your word is my rule." "What about Paul? You mentioned finding him?"

"At last! I'd gone for a ramble through the fish markets, which were gleaming with fresh catch and crowded with buyers and flaneurs, even though it was early on a Sunday morning. I recognized Paul at once—I recognized a twin. He was standing among a small group of locals gathered around a steaming pot half as big as an oil drum, from which a vendor was spooning out small blobs that his customers swallowed with relish. I could not identify them until I was close by: baby octopuses boiled in their broth. I ate two. To no one in particular I offered to provide a bottle of white wine to complete our pleasure. There was a murmur of assent. I soon returned from the nearest hostelry with a bottle of muscadet and half a dozen glasses. After identifying ourselves, Paul went off to buy himself a pint of McEwan's (he told me he had no liking for wine), and I went with him. I insisted on paying for his beer; it was a welcome occasion to introduce myself. I told him I had been hoping to meet him since I had arrived. I would explain why later; this was perhaps not the moment to be talking business."

Berenice: "What *is* your business? At least your business with him?" "It's true you know nothing about me except what my sister looks like. I had a chance to tell Paul, but I wasted it. I did hear a lot about *his* business. No sooner had I mentioned that my interest in him was professional than he took me firmly in hand. He turned us away from our little group and the glittering heaps of fish and led me to the docks nearby, where he put me (unquestioned and unquestioning—he correctly assumed that I knew he dealt in textiles) aboard a fifteen-foot, square-sterned skiff powered by an outboard motor. It bore us efficiently to the little island six hundred yards out in the bay—you've undoubtedly noticed it. On the way, Paul told me that on his journey here he had found himself in the company of two men from the Levant, a father and son named Mehmed and Ahmet; they had long lived in communities of spinners and weavers, they had even worked with a master rugmaker. 'Meeting them seemed like a stroke of luck, and I've always taken my luck seriously. I told them of my trade and offered them the option of coming to work for me if they needed jobs. They did. You are about to see them in action.'

"Paul was beginning to interest me in ways I hadn't foreseen. I can't say I liked him. He made no effort to be like-able, but forthrightness isn't necessarily a fault. Approaching the island, I saw that there were no buildings except for one large wooden structure—his 'modest factory.' Paul explained that he had converted it from what used to be a fisherman's refuge-*cum*-depot. He had done this work immaculately, as was evident even in the little yard that preceded the factory proper. Any ravages of time and random visitors had been expunged. Inside, the walls had been neatly repainted, and the various machines placed in a way that allowed easy access to them and left the overall space uncrowded and almost elegant, clearly a labor of love, and of some underlying commitment to the perfectibility of work. In the second room Mehmed and Ahmet were busy at their tasks, so busy that Paul refrained from interrupting them. Aside from one rapid glance, concentrated on what they were doing, they paid no attention to us anyway.

"Paul immediately began explaining their purpose in what soon became mind-numbing detail. A preparatory cloth had already been made from two different kinds of fleece washed and mordanted with madder, weld, and pomegranate skins and combined into denser fabric than either wool could form alone. Ahmet had cut this colored cloth into ornamental shapes that he then laid on the floor on mats of appropriate size assembled from local reeds, onto which Mehmed, using a forked cherry-wood tool called a *cubuk*, was now tossing clumps of carded wool with prodigious accuracy. Paul then launched into a description of what would happen subsequently, but this I will spare you. In fact I spared myself as much of it as I decently could, pretexting an appointment in town that I thought was invention but which became real enough soon after Paul had returned me to shore (a providential east wind made further talk impossible): meeting you. I'm happy to have been in time for that. There you were, standing out of the wind in the shade of your parasol, I walked up to you as though I'd known you forever, the woman I'd longed for since the dawn of time."

2

John and Paul were also visitors to the town. They were twins, as identical as can be. They wore the same clothes, chino trousers and open-neck sweaters, in John's case adorned with a faded maroon neckerchief. Both were addicted to the shellfish harvested year-round from the rocks and sands of the coast: little clams, winkles, cockles, crabs, and above all sea urchins—their dessert, as both said. They drank only McEwan's India pale ale and smoked the same thin black Brazilian cigars. They drove identical cars, beige postwar Dyna-Panhards from France, indistinguishable except by their license plates. Neither ventured out late in the evening: they were hard workers, Paul at his island factory, John off long before dawn as mate on a fishing boat, where he earned good wages and an enviable reputation. Each had taken lodgings in rather shabby boarding houses. Each read the *International Herald Tribune*, sent by mail; never—at least in public—a book of any sort. Their intonation and accent afforded no key to their identities, although they said very different things. The only clues were John's neckerchief and his occasional wearing of wire-rimmed reading glasses.

Their boarding houses lay far apart, at opposite sides of the town. John attended the Methodist church, Paul the Roman Catholic. They drank their pale ale at different bars. They were in fact never seen together and apparently avoided all commerce with one another. This puzzled but did not disturb the native inhabitants—"an odd story" was the general remark on their relationship, or the lack of one. John and Paul had been accepted on their own terms by the community: John being accounted the more genial of the two, Paul's tendency to gruffness excused as a sign of seriousness; and, of course, his bringing his small industry to the town counted in his favor.

"Won't *you* tell me, Andreas, what you think of them? For starters, what *is* your secretive business with Paul?" "There's nothing secretive about it—it's simply that the subject never came up before. I've never mentioned my politics either, or my favorite books or operas. Between sweet love-making and sweet sleep (at least speaking for myself) ..." "Yes, that is a trait of perfect manliness!" "... we've had little enough time for conversation. So I shall tell you now: I am by profession a publisher, a very modest one, where I am the sole editor, my only employee being a secretary—more an indentured servant, but I overwork her in the kindest way and make up in attentiveness and sympathy for her minute wages. I regret not making more than a sufficient but careful living. No best sellers, which is a shame. No: it isn't. My joy is in publishing books I like, and I know that's a lucky privilege in my line of work.

"When I heard about John and Paul, I thought that theirs was a story that should be told; best of all by them. Not the story of their similarities—fascinating enough but no surprise to anyone the least bit familiar with the lore of identical twins—but the story of their obstinate separation from one another, something hardly imaginable. Ideally, an account by each of them would be the best, but I realized that initiating such a project would inevitably make me an actor in their relationship, whether for good or bad—it has become almost a scientific cliché that one cannot 'objectively' evaluate a question without modifying its givens, something I earnestly hope to avoid. So it would have to be one or the other who told the tale, at least initially; and from all I was able to glean about their temperaments, Paul struck me as the better choice. I was afraid John's reputedly generous nature would tinge with sentiment whatever might be dark and difficult in their relation; whereas Paul's openly stubborn, bluff drive had something of a juggernaut in it, meaning less caution and more frankness in his account. What I saw of him today seemed to confirm my intuition. We'll see. I'm here in any case to try and convince him to write his version of events. It should be a great occasion if he accepts."

"Thank you. I heartily agree. Now I must tell you at once that I too came here because of them, although with no purpose as practical as yours. As you may have guessed, I am a professional psychologist, of the behaviorist school. I study and teach how and why people do what they do independently of their feelings and will. It's not only genetics. Think of my uncle's ginger poodle." (If Andreas let the reference pass without a smile, it was also without irritation.) "The behavior of identical twins has long exerted a fascination on those in my profession—and, darling Andreas, I must confess that I am hopelessly fascinated by people's behavior, and not only in my work—I go around peering at the habitants of our world and at every step my scientific precautions desert me.

"And these two! They're not conducting themselves the way they're supposed to! When I first read about identical twins, perhaps in the same journals you did, impetuous curiosity, and a desire to observe and, if I could, know them, started worrying my brain and my nerves. Why this compulsive separation of two lives that are in agreement about virtually everything? Can they be happy? If not, why did they both settle in the same distant little town? What might I do for them if ever they confided in me? (I admit to that unlikely dream.) So I'm here for no reason but the impression—a distant impression—gleaned or more likely fantasized from anonymous gray printed matter. And I expect that in the end there will be nothing to show for this expense of enthusiasm. Except you."

"I do hope and pray that 'we' last. How did you meet John? You're half way, let me point out, to realizing your first wish."

"On my way into town I stopped at a café just past the upper road. It's in a run-down neighborhood, which sets it off effectively—its freshly painted shutters, well-polished brasses, its general cleanliness and gaiety of note. It is pleasantly run. It offers acceptable wines and good coffee, of which I was drinking a cup when John unexpectedly accosted me and asked if he could sit for a moment at my table. Of course I said yes, trying not to show my pleasure. He spoke to me most gently, at first asking me obvious questions: When had I arrived here? How long was I planning to stay? I suspect he is attracted to older women. (I spoke of you as soon as I could tactfully do so.) We soon went on to less obvious matters, a conversation that after half an hour or so led to his eulogy of feelings, remember? To which he may have been helped by the wine we were by then drinking. I liked him extremely and am glad to think he liked me too. I made no mention of Paul. Next time, perhaps."

"Congratulations! *My* feelings are: singly we may know only one of them, together we know them both. It's a start. What wine were you drinking?" "Sardinian Vermentino." "Excellent. What do we do now? I thought of dropping a note at Paul's lodgings and asking him to have dinner with me, or with us, as you think best." "Shall I ask John to join us?" "Given what we know of them, he'll surely refuse. In time maybe, when they know us better." "I suppose you're right. By the way, the Hydes have asked us to dine with them to-morrow evening. We'll see what they have to say about our young men." "I fear I know all to well what they'll say. In the meantime I suggest that we draw up a list of subjects—books, politics, and so forth—to start filling in the blanks of what we don't know about one another." "If you like. I must say I think it's a silly plan. Whenever I'm asked such questions— say, what books do I like?—I invariably forget the Brontës. Furthermore, it's a way of sowing the seeds of potential dis-cord. If you're a royalist and I'm a communist—well, we must swear never to argue." "I swear it will never matter to me. *Are* you a communist?" "Not at the moment. I'm simply a slave of Eros." "Please don't get over it. Do you know the song, 'Love is sweeping the country'?" "I'm adding it to my favorites, if songs appear as a category on your list of blanks."

3

Geoffrey Hyde was saying, "Certainly there's something odd behind the twins' relationship, but I can't begin to imagine what."

Berenice and Andreas had walked the half mile to the Hydes' house. On their previous visit they had found the front door locked, without bell or knocker. This time it lay invitingly open, and they had walked straight in to a cheerful welcome from their hosts. They were now at table, enjoying the main course: baked fish, locally called hunting horn, white-fleshed and strong-flavored, garnished simply with salt, pepper, and olive oil. With it they drank a chilled *aligoté* burgundy from the Côte Chalonnaise.

To Andreas's ears, Geoffrey's comment on the twins only echoed the town's opinion. Margot shook her head rather somberly and half demurred: "I find their behavior more than a little upsetting." Berenice asked, "Because it was such a scare?" "Oh no, not a scare. The way they made places for themselves in the community was so natural and, well, elegant. Hardly scary. It's the utter unlikeliness of their attitude towards one another that bothers me—saddens me, actually." "Have you come to know them at all?" "Not really. Geoffrey sees Paul from time to time in his position as the town's economic supervisor—what is your official title, dear? I'm never sure of getting it right." "'Mercantile Assessor for the Borough.' It dates from an earlier age." Andreas: "And when you assume your function, how are you to be addressed? Mr. Assessor? Mr. Mercantile Assessor? Mr. Mercantile Assessor for the Borough?" "Geoffrey usually, frequently Jeff." "I mean," Margot continued, "they never even communicate, or not in any detectable way." "That's not quite true, Margot. They do share one very visible companion, who might well act as a go-between."

At this Andreas perked up. "Aha! Who is that?" "He probably means Wicheria, accented on the second syllable, I believe." Geoffrey: "Who else?" "And who is Wicheria?" Berenice asked. It was almost the tone of hope. "She is our one-woman bohemia," Geoffrey replied. "She wears outlandish clothes, like green velvet pantaloons and musketeer boots, if you see what I mean. She often dyes her long full hair a kind of dark smoldering red. Her smile fairly glitters. She is in fact almost beautiful, in her mildly provocative way." Then, with a slight change of voice, "I approve of her completely." Margot added, "Do you know Charley Kipper? Our captain of police. He told us that after a clique of old farts insisted he investigate the young woman, he had found her innocent of any hint of troublemaking. She does not traffic in drugs. She does not peddle her charms. She does not pilfer. She does not pursue married men, or wealthy ones. She simply expresses her love of life in a slightly provocative way."

Geoffrey: "She has a most beautiful laugh. It starts in the bass register, but as it rises through her body it also rises in pitch, until it spills from her mouth in a diminuendo of short, bright sighs."

Like Berenice, Andreas had followed this exchange attentively. He asked, "You said John and Paul 'shared' Wicheria. What does that mean?" "It's an ambiguous word that I probably shouldn't have used. Both John and Paul are friendly with her, perhaps even close friends. They are often seen with her, separately of course, having dinner and on rare occasions at the Hunting Horn, our 'palais de la danse.' The girl dances uproariously, leaping, twirling, her red mane swinging around her head in keeping with a general air of witchiness that was apparently the source of her nickname. When they dance with her, Paul keeps to his more measured if acceptably up-to-date movements. John does his best to follow his partner's gyrations, or if he doesn't follow, at least mimics them." Margot: "I've always considered this a token of his charming tact." Andreas: "Have you spoken to her about them?" Geoffrey: "I feel that it's wiser for someone in an official position not to show curiosity about private affairs. In any case, I hardly know Wicheria well enough to question her about her friends." "Yes, that's more to the point," Margot concluded.

On the walk back, Berenice took Andreas's arm, less out of tenderness than for support. The evening had left her dizzy. She had kept all her intense fantasies concerning the twins intact, but her knowledge of them was still minimal: there was a gap between these extremes like an unmapped pit. She felt she was coming home not from her neighbors' but from the shore below, or from a day spent on the ocean, or from some place at the end of the world. She exclaimed, "Do those boys really exist?" Andreas answered, "The story will tell. It's taking an operatic turn, isn't it?"

What did he mean? He stopped them on a bridge crossing a little brook and they listened to the water warbling. "Sometimes," she went on, "I feel this place doesn't exist either." "Then we're making it up rather well. But we're still only spectators." They walked on through the night toward their bed.

4

The following week Berenice and Andreas in turn invited the Hydes for dinner. Berenice served local fare: smoked red mullet from the Kaufmann smoke house, a shoulder of lamb from the inland highlands (so imbued with the wild thyme and savory it had grazed on, it scarcely needed further seasoning), string beans and salad from their garden, goat cheese, sautéd sweet apples. The wines were imported: Alsatian Pinot Blanc, Morgon from the Beaujolais, nonvintage champagne. They had reached the apples and champagne when Andreas suggested a way they might continue the evening.

"We may not know each other well, but we do seem to get along. My guess is that we'd enjoy knowing each other better—I certainly would, and I think I've found a way of doing that that would be easy and even entertaining. My idea is that each of us take turns telling a story. Not necessarily stories about ourselves, although obviously there's nothing wrong with that, but also stories we've heard from other people, or remember from books and plays. Stories that we'd love to tell or retell ourselves or, perhaps more accurately, that we'd love to *hear* told. Even stories made up out of whole cloth, why not? All that's up to the narrator. The one thing that I'd ask of you is not to choose a story because you think it will impress the rest of us. Let the story choose you! What do you think?"

Margot: "I think it's a great idea. I *love* stories." Geoffrey: "It makes me a little nervous. Will I have to produce mine this evening?" Andreas: "I imagined one story at a time. I hope we'll be having more dinners." Margot: "Of course we will." Berenice: "That way you'll all have time to prepare, like me— as a forewarned hostess I thought I'd go first. O.K.?" There were no objections.

"This is the story of one man, a 'man's man,' a professional valet and a good one. I didn't witness most of what I'm about to tell you, only one evening towards the end after I'd been called in in a professional capacity.

"The valet's name was Hubert. He felt great esteem for his employer, and discreet but genuine affection as well. He did everything in his power to satisfy his master's small needs and see that he was kept neatly elegant for his social and professional engagements. Hubert enjoyed his work, which— conscientious as he was—kept him as busy as he could wish. He was given every other Sunday off, as well as any workday evening when the gentleman he served had no need of him.

"On a Sunday in late March, a sunny Sunday full of portents of the nascent spring, Hubert arrived by streetcar in the center of the sizable city where he had always lived. He got off at a stop opposite the main entrance of Fosdick Park, the largest in town. As he stepped to the curb, he at once became aware of a sensation that would gradually envelope him, and would subsequently haunt him for the rest of his life.

"The spring sun was hot, the air was still—utterly still. There was not the breath of a breeze. It wasn't only that no leaf or blade of grass so much as quivered: something like an inverse wind had apparently emptied the air of its invisible stuff and fixed leaves and grass in an immobility as absolute as that of a photograph. A ways inside the park, Hubert felt himself sucked into a comparable equilibrium—he could still move without the slightest hesitation, but he sensed, moving or not, packets of an indefinable substance falling away from him into the weightless air, first from the skin of his limbs (calves, small of back, shoulders), then from muscles (slender triceps, stubborn hamstring), from stiff bones (knee caps), and even from his brain and its subversive nerves, until at the end a bar of steel that stretched from shoulder to shoulder across his sternum, of which he had never been aware, was gently lifted from him. This released a spurt of joy, also unsuspected grief upwelling, so as he delightedly smiled, tears rolled down his cheeks to drench his chest. He hid behind a tree so as not to be seen crying. He raised his arms as if in salute, not of any god, idea, or force of nature, just the unnamable source of his release. He quickly thought: 'I have to tell the world about this.'

"Still tingling with weightlessness, on his way home he reminded himself, 'I should let people know,' and already a seed of doubt dropped into his mind. He could never realize this wish, he admitted—at least not alone: alone he would be merely a ranting idiot. He needed at least one person beside him who had shared, or at least believed in, his improbable experience; that would give him a first semblance of plausibility, which he might then develop. But how could he win over this first disciple? Why should *anyone* believe him? Why should he have been chosen for such exotic joy?

"Hubert was not alone for long. One person in the Sunday park had noticed him; she never quite understood why, or why she kept watching him and so witnessing a transfiguration that bewildered and intrigued her. A small, slender man, fine-featured but less than handsome, was slowly invested before her eyes with a visible ecstasy that had no visible cause. She did not understand, but he radiated such happiness as made her yearn to partake of his feelings. When he left the park, she walked after him, took the same streetcar as he, and followed him all the way home.

"Her name was Rachel. Comely, not tall or short, her head capped with auburn curls, her body compact, lithe, and soft. That day she wore a yellow blouse, blue jeans, and penny loafers. She worked in a scholarly bookstore, selling the works of Spinoza, Walser, and Groddeck to 'serious' readers young and old. She lived alone in a very small flat near the university.

"Hubert had disappeared through a back door of the house where he lived. She walked up to the door and knocked on it firmly. There was no response, the door was unlocked, she walked into a kind of shadowy storeroom (racks of bottles and fruit) that led to a large, bright kitchen. A plump middle-aged woman put down the celery stalks she had been chopping and turned to face Rachel with not unfriendly surprise. Rachel: 'Forgive me for barging in, but a gentleman was here a moment ago—I don't know his name, but I need to speak

to him, if he would consent to receive me. I'm Rachel Au-
erbach—that will mean nothing to him.' 'And I am Rosina.
Please to be seated. I go to make him know you are here.
Without doubt he will be content in the company of such a
pretty young lady.' Exit Rosina.

"A few minutes later she returned with Hubert. '*Signor* Hubert, here is *Signorina* Rachel.' Rachel apologized for seeming
impudent: she summed up her observations in the park and
her curiosity to learn what was going on. Hubert: 'We can
talk in the servants' sitting-room. Please excuse us, Rosina.'
'Naturally. Ought I to make tea?' 'Coffee, perhaps—and for
you, Miss Rachel?' 'Oh yes, coffee for me, too.'

"When they were settled, Rachel asked, 'Are you really a
servant?' 'Very much so: valet to the master of the house, a
distinguished gentleman, Sir Bellamy Boyens. A very kind
man, too, and his wife, Constance, an equally kind woman.
Not perhaps kind enough, either of them, to appreciate my fit
this afternoon.' 'It didn't look like a fit.' 'I'm very glad you've
come. Did *you* notice anything peculiar about the place?' 'I
did notice the stillness. Unfortunately it didn't affect me like
it did you. I didn't guess it was what had stirred you.' 'But
you've guessed it now!'

"Rachel began to feel that they were concocting a very
Jamesian situation. Since he was still 'off' that evening, Hubert suggested they dine together. She accepted. Afterwards
he in turn accepted her invitation to take her home, where
he stayed till break of day.

"So their love affair began, and their alliance. She was thirty-
three, he fifty-one; he was a bearer of new truth revealed, she

his disciple and scholiast; but differences of years and roles became no more than complements to their unpredicted, passionate love.

"His employers couldn't help noticing a change in Hubert: his nightlong absences whenever he was excused from his duties were accompanied by his evolution from pleasant and conscientious helper into a confident, virile individual, his somewhat drawn features and pale complexion filling out with almost ruddy healthfulness.

"One day Constance asked Hubert to join her for a private talk in the living room. She had him sit next to her on the sofa by the window overlooking the garden. She began by emphasizing how sincerely she and Bellamy were fond of him: there had been so many years of steadfast loyalty on his part, during which he had revealed his generous, thoughtful character in a multitude of small but eloquent contributions to their lives. Of late they had recognized a shift in his comportment: a shift towards happiness, or so they felt, which they could only welcome. Constance confessed they were also itching with wonder. What had happened? She begged him to confide in her. She promised not to object to anything he told her—no, she wanted to back him to the hilt.

"Perhaps Hubert's sense of decorum may have been troubled by Constance's words; he could not help being moved by them. He consented to her request, relating how one Sunday afternoon he had undergone a strong, strange interior experience that had somehow been observed by a person unknown to him—a younger woman who was curious enough to follow him here: she was intelligent and charming. They had quickly fallen in love. He hoped his infatuation had not affected the quality of his service, which was as ever the cornerstone of his life.

"Constance exclaimed, 'Not any more it isn't! I shall tell Bellamy what you just told me. I now tenderly implore you to let us meet your young lady. Tea tomorrow afternoon, perhaps?'

"So Rachel was invited into the household, first to tea, soon after to dinner; at which Bellamy asked if she had secretarial talents. Rachel answered that she typed well enough and she could learn shorthand if that should be necessary. 'It won't be. I just need help getting out from underneath the paperwork that's cluttering my life. I can pay you more than what you earn selling books. What do you say?' Constance then added, 'And we can cede you and Hubert the second guest room. He will thus be relieved of having to scurry away nights to wherever it is you live.' Until then Rachel had been a model of courtesy and demureness; she now cried a little. 'Yes, yes— you do agree, darling Hubert?' He replied with a laugh of astonishment—his old life and new life were suddenly one."

Margot asked if Hubert hadn't taken the place of the son the Boeyens never had. "Oh, they had a son, but he'd gone off on his own while still a young man. He wanted to start a publishing house. Bellamy did not approve." Andreas held his tongue.

"A colleague at the bookshop agreed to take over the lease on Rachel's apartment, so that within days she brought her clothes and a capacious trunkload of books to her new home. She began her work with Sir Bellamy immediately, determined to quickly learn how she could best save him time and bother. This soon led to her accepting responsibility for nearly all his activities insofar as they involved writing:

editing much private and most professional correspondence, paying bills, drafting proposals, speeches, and articles—she loved it all, exploring a world that she had heretofore regarded as foreign and vaguely threatening. Occasionally she found time to help Constance in the cutting garden, or in planning her menus. And if she had finished her work for the day, she joined Rosina in the kitchen to help prepare the evening's dinner. She and Hubert spent happy days, their paths often crossing as they busily plied their respective tasks, and happy nights in their bigger bed."

Berenice interrupted her tale with a sigh. "I wish I could stop right here. But a story must be as true to itself as any fiction.

"There was, after all, a third strand in Hubert's life that the Boyens' generosity couldn't immediately benefit: his ardent wish, actually more of a tyrannical obsession, to somehow transmit to his fellow human beings his inspiring experience in the park. This was a project that Rachel was eager to abet. He had spoken cautiously to Constance and Bellamy about what had happened. They had listened encouragingly, but with no sign of recognizing the magnitude of the experience in Hubert's life.

"With Rachel, Hubert at first tried to determine places and times where the original conditions of his revelation might reappear (its effect on him was still vivid). They studied weather reports and forecasts, they took trips to places near their town where windless sunshine was predicted. They found only very faint winds and pleasant warmth, never the 'reverse wind' that immobilized the air and all it touched.

This was no way to bring Hubert's new cognizance to the world.

"They sought professional help. They called on communicators in various fields, teachers, priests and pastors, publicists, journalists, theater people. Since the two of them were serious and polite, most of those consulted listened to them and then invariably tried to enroll them in their own work. The teachers invited them to participate in their seminars (that is, work as unpaid assistants); the holy men urged them to convert; publicists insisted the couple hire them; journalists looked for a story. Hubert and Rachel also wrote to noted iconoclasts in other fields—R. D. Laing, for instance, and Werner Erhard, then living in England. The 'antipsychiatrist' hailed Hubert's story as further evidence of the primacy of personal experience. The founder of est recognized their need as a familiar one: he recommended creating a succession of artificial situations that would stimulate sensations and feelings like Hubert's. He thought it would help if they grounded their work on a firm, if discreet, philosophical basis, the way Plato in the dialogue called *Meno* justified his teaching a young slave geometry by the mechanics of anamnesis.

"Neither Hubert nor Rachel had such precise knowledge of philosophy and knew better than to try acquiring it now. They decided to apply Erhard's suggestion utilizing simple description. With Sir Bellamy's help, they found a small auditorium they could rent by the day; they had a flyer printed announcing the presentation of a personal 'life experience' that they considered 'highly interesting and potentially useful to anyone with an open mind.' They placed the flyer in neighborhood shops and restaurants. Constance sent invitations to friends she felt might respond favorably—in doing this her expectations were low, but she encouraged their guests with the reassurance that she and Bellamy would both attend.

"So it was that at six o'clock on a weekday evening twelve people were assembled in the rather bleak room that Sir Bellamy had rented. Constance had brightened it up with vases of chrysanthemums set on either end of the long table behind which Rachel and Hubert were seated. The audience consisted of Constance and Bellamy, three of their friends, and—presumably drawn by the flyer—three down-at-heels middle-aged persons as well as a couple about twenty years old, well-dressed in the untraditional fashion of the decade.

"Rachel was the first to address the gathering, briefly relating the background of the present event, then presenting Hubert at greater length and testifying to his sincerity and the esteem in which she held him.

"Rachel spoke well: simply and cheerfully. This could not be said of Hubert. His nature was compounded of discretion and shyness, and genuine modesty, too; never before had he been in a position where his own life was set center stage. He swallowed his words or tripped over them; he could not hide the embarrassment that possessed him. Rachel tried prompting him, but it made no difference. A restless boredom descended on the Boeyens' guests and the middle-aged strangers. Constance and Bellamy themselves felt a quirky mixture of sadness and irritation. Only the young couple remained attentive, smiling, sometimes giggling and making encouraging noises. When Hubert shamefacedly ended his talk, the young pair's vigorous applause stood out from the desultory clapping of the others. As the meeting broke up, Constance heard the young woman say to her companion, 'They're right—the world has got to be let in on this.' Constance wasn't sure of the tone in which these words were spoken.

"Two more presentations were scheduled, one on each of the following weeks. After doing what they could to reassure Hubert that his fiasco was not definitive, Rachel and the Boeyens insisted that he prepare diligently for these appearances. Bellamy had made numerous speeches in his time, obviously not of this sort, but he had learned some basic rules. 'Write out what you want to say and reread it until you have the shape of it in your bones. If you have to, jot down notes that you can glance at while you're speaking to keep yourself on track. Above all, *rehearse.*'

"Hubert did his best to follow this advice. It helped, but not much.

"The audience at the second event was unlike the first, and bigger: over twenty seats were filled. The young couple had enrolled many of their friends, who like them called themselves 'hip' or 'cool.' They received Rachel's introduction with sympathetic smiles. When Hubert began narrating his experience in the park, the smiles changed gradually but inexorably to laughter, gentle at first, then filled with a kind of incredulous enthusiasm. For some reason these young adults found the account of Hubert shedding the weight that encased him totally hilarious. They weren't antagonistic, they cheered him on with little bursts of applause, and at the end showered him with bravos and whistles.

"Hubert naturally didn't know what to make of this. He had pretty much succeeded in following his text to the end, but his 'success' left him dumbfounded.

"It was after this event that I was called in by a team of local psychologists, contacted by Bellamy, who was worried by Hubert's growing confusion and discouragement. I met Rachel, who briefed me on what had happened. I then attended the third and final session. It drew a still larger attendance than the week before, and among the newcomers an element appeared that was no less exuberant than its forerunners but less kind. I felt they had come to jeer as well as laugh; and jeer they did. The low point was reached when Hubert told of the weird packets falling from his bones, and a thinly bearded young man shouted, 'Hey, Hube! Did you get your rocks off, too?' This garnered a small laugh from the crowd, not from Hubert, who turned white, rose to his feet, and started shrieking obscenities at his heckler. For a while he stood there, stamping one foot compulsively on the platform, until Rachel summarily ended the meeting, leading Hubert past cheering spectators into the cooler air outside. I followed them.

"Rachel led us to a restaurant nearby. We ordered a stiff whisky for Hubert, and for us, too. We tried to make him eat; we pampered him with whatever words we thought might soothe him. I made a remark that I've regretted ever since. 'Hubert, you said what you wanted to say, and some day your words may get through to them. That does happen. In the meantime you made them laugh. That's not dishonorable. It's a commonplace joy, but a real one.' Hubert said, 'I came to speak to them as a modest evangelist, not to be their clown.'

"That was pretty much the end for Hubert. Rachel was dismayed that not only had he been stripped of his zeal in spreading his 'good word,' but there remained not a trace of the excitement of his original experience, not even a consoling memory. He sank into carnivorous melancholy, with its attendant petty monsters—insomnia by night, constipation, back ache, and migraine by day. He became skeletally thin and brutally rude. Melancholy is inaccessible to psychotherapy, so he was treated with chemicals that only damped down his agitation into resigned sullenness.

"The Boeyens at last decided they could no longer keep him under their roof. They found and paid for a rest home in the outskirts of the city in which he could take early retirement. It was a reasonably good solution: Hubert found himself in new surroundings where nothing reminded him of his disappointments, aside from Rachel's visits.

"She visited him almost every day. She could not quite cheer him up, but she brought him rudimentary peace of mind. They still loved one another, and each somehow knew that reestablishing their former intimacy meant risking havoc.

"On clement days they took walks together in the nearby countryside. Once, in early autumn, they went by bus as far as the mountain range that lay east of the city. The mountains were low, with gentle grades; the pair ascended one not much higher than a big hill. They nevertheless reached a height above the last grassy slopes where no vegetation grew. Around them stretched an expanse of dark gray limestone streaked with thin fissures that rain had incised in its downward flow. It was a quiet afternoon, in fact an absolutely silent one. Hubert remembered a remark of Webern's to the effect that no matter how complete the surrounding silence, one could always distinguish some sound, however faint. Leaning against the high limestone that flanked the path, putting a hand on Rachel's arm to keep her still, he listened hard— could that be a far-off crow? As soon as he heard it, it faded. There was not even a whisper of wind. The rain of centuries had been sucked into the limestone's clefts. Rachel was smiling a peculiar smile that reminded him of something. Holding out his hands to her, he asked, "Is it happening? To you?" Rachel took his hands in hers and kissed them, raising glazed eyes in the fading light. No tears for Rachel; she knew that she was about to spin straight up into the twilit sky. He had to take her word for it—he himself felt nothing much but faint, overdue relief.

"Next day he said to her, 'Now we have our holy order. A society of two. That's enough room to stand up in.'

"Rachel and I had become friends. Her letters keep me up to date. The most recent one arrived last Saturday to inform me that, a week before his sixtieth birthday, Hubert had died. He was clear-headed, calm, slightly disgusted."

Margot asked, "Didn't this fellow have any family?" "He had a twin brother. He'd emigrated years before all this. Now I *must* go to bed. Good night."

5

Berenice had been sincere in saying she "had to go to bed," but it was not, as one might expect, because of fatigue. When Andreas eventually followed her upstairs, he found her wide awake and eager to chat.

"You aren't Bellamy's son, by some prank of fate? His given name was Lewis, I believe." "So was mine. I decided to change half my identity—my half. I had nothing against my family, after all. Does it matter?" "Only that we came so close." "You mean all that time wasted? Years of love foregone? My darling, but who knows what disasters such 'convenient' intimacy might have brought down on us? What could be better than this? I'll take contingency any day over a family connection." Berenice agreed. She also wondered if, by her rough calculation, close to three thousand lost nights of erotic plenitude didn't justify at least a whisper of regret.

Ever since they had realized they were in this town for the same reason, Berenice and Andreas had agreed they must arrange meetings together with each of the twins, much longer and better targeted ones than their single encounters. Paul should come first, since he was the one that Andreas hoped would write the twins' joint biography. Since visiting Paul's factory, Andreas had kept minimally in touch with him, through emails and sometimes a note left at his boarding house. It was through such a note that Paul was invited to have dinner with Andreas and Berenice; Paul was asked to choose the date and restaurant.

On an evening in early October the three of them met at the bistro Paul had picked—Barr's Grill, "the best meat in town," Paul announced. "At the moment I'm recovering from an overdose of surf and surf." "And they surely carry McEwan's Export," Andreas added. Paul smiled pleasantly.

Pleasant smile or not, Andreas knew that he must stick to the approach that he and Berenice had agreed on: Andreas would make no reference to his plan of enrolling Paul as an author until the three of them had shared a meal and enough time together to establish at least a decor of familiarity. Berenice made sure that Paul's plate was kept full; Andreas monitored the refills of his favorite Scottish ale. Both of them were professionally experienced in spinning agreeable conversation with strangers whose cooperation they needed—Andreas having to soothe an author's impatience with publication delays, Beatrice connecting to a child with Down syndrome.

They kept the focus of the conversation on Paul. Since he had already talked shop with him, Andreas took the lead in inquiring about his work; but Beatrice had her moment, too. She asked Paul for news of "Mehmed and Ahmet, or is it Mehmet and Ahmed, I know I'm hopeless with Arab names."

Paul: "You had it right the first time. They're both fine—they like our ways. They don't even mind that there's no mosque." He was happy to talk about his business. He volunteered an account of his education, too, since it was so important in preparing him for his career.

"I was lucky. From the age of six to seventeen I boarded (there were family problems) at a school called Newell Academy, a really good place. It was there I completed my primary and secondary classes. They taught a broadly traditional curriculum in mathematics, literature, and world history (including cultural history)—it wasn't quite classical—I had small Latin and *no* Greek—but it was mind-expanding all the same. Better than that: since many of the school's pupils came from poor families, it made sure that if any subject had practical extensions, they too would be taught. The history of architecture was complemented by courses in carpentry, masonry, basic engineering. Our study of the industrial revolution included mechanics and the first principles of running a business.

"The idea was that any graduate of the school would be able to find himself a decent job without too much sweat. In big cities, where good plumbers and carpenters were rare, a diploma as a pipe fitter or a cabinet maker ensured a starting wage. Smart prison inmates knew this; so did the directors of Newell Academy. Manual workers also relished being freed at least from the tyranny of respectable clothing (jacket, shirt, and tie)—a man in overalls with a hammer looped to his hip could enter a gentleman's club without raising an eyebrow.

"I'd guess a good third of my class could write computer code by the time they left. Not me—I went for construction and business savvy. I had additional luck in catching the attention of a teacher called Ned Linnen, an architect by trade. He thought I had promise. He made sure I was on top of all my subjects (meaning any hint of slacking brought him down on me hard) and he helped me along whenever he could. He told me one day, 'You'll probably have to earn your living by selling something, and to succeed at that you have to master a few basic constants with invariable rules, whether you're selling encyclopedias or sardines: inventory, logistics, marketing, things like that—when you can manage these, you've got a chance.'

"I was accepted by three good universities when I graduated, but I wasn't interested. I wanted to test myself in the commercial world. After twelve years and a bit, I can say I've done OK. I started off as a bricklayer. It's a tough trade, and I was very good at it, working mainly on big municipal projects, learning all I could about how buildings actually get built.

"Ned Linnen sent me to see a well-known architect who took me under his wing, and I went on learning. It was with him that I got interested in textiles, which he used in clever new ways. So when I'd saved enough money to start my own business, which was essentially the same one that I set up here, it was manufacturing and selling textiles for architectural use. Most of my big jobs are commissioned abroad. Two months ago I was able to buy up a couple of hundred bales of Thai silk on the cheap, lots of different colors. I cut them up and reassembled them in abstract designs of my own and sold them to a retail bank in Ljubljana to line the walls of their reception areas. I do all right locally, too—I've woven curtains and carpets in a soothing shade of mauve for the waiting room of our clinic. And I've made a killing with my first venture into fashion." "Fashion?" Berenice asked. "I wish I'd known. There were a few fiendishly hot summer days when I dreamt of gauze djellabahs." "No, nothing that elaborate. But you see the couple sitting at the bar? See what they're wearing on their heads?" "Kepi Kaps!" Andreas exclaimed. "They're all over the place. You make them?" "When you came out to the island, you saw Mehmed and Ahmet starting the process—conditioning the felt. A soft kepi! Who could have guessed?" Berenice: "The faded orange and black are delicious. And the forward tilt makes pretty women prettier." Paul: "Andreas, what did you mean, way back—you thought we might work together?"

"Of course. I'll explain.

"Like you, I went out on my own early, although I did put in three years at university—I'd have done better at Newell Academy. All that my studies did for me was get me hooked on literature—not as a writer but as a reader, and there was no 'practical counterpart' for that! I decided to start a publishing house so that I could commission books that I wanted to read but didn't yet exist. I didn't know the first thing about business—selling was something I had to learn on the job. I did have the sense to spend a year as an apprentice with an established distributor, where I got to know something of the nuts and bolts of the book trade. After that I managed to wangle a couple of grants, one from a state agency, another from a private foundation, and brandishing these, I approached my bank—a perfectly respectable bank!—and actually secured a loan from them. I helped all this happen by displaying my college record and behaving as though I were a well-connected gent; my family was distinguished all right, but I kept them completely out of it. I was happy to have raised some capital by myself, although it depressed me to think that society's finances were in the hands of such susceptible incompetents and that in my own small way I was aggravating a situation of general economic decay.

"No matter—I was on my own, and I survived. I rented office space. I engaged a secretary, a good-natured young woman of considerable intelligence who had no idea what she was in for. My year at the distributor had acquainted me with the names of many contemporary writers and what might be expected of them. My university acquaintances, efficiently climbing the hierarchies of the liberal professions, provided a network that made it relatively easy for me to contact the writers who interested me. You see, I was not looking to publish literature as it's commonly thought of—no novels, certainly no poetry or plays. Imagination, yes—but imagination demonstrated in the way unusual people chose or were forced to live their lives, and those lives duly recorded by others if necessary but best by themselves."

Paul, at this point, was no longer smiling. He had assumed a markedly sullen aspect, that as he listened to Andreas grew only glummer.

Andreas: "This was my one strength: I knew what I wanted, and I quickly learned how to get it. There were objective factors to exploit. At the time I started publishing, most writers were being paid pitifully little. I offered contracts that were generous in the long term: small advances but royalties at almost twice the going rate. I could afford this because thanks to the computer, production costs were low, I had only one employee to pay, and I could use direct advertising to promote my books. The arrangement also encouraged writers to produce something saleable.

"And it worked. Luck no doubt played a part—I'm all for that! We brought out a number of interesting works. An in-depth account of Raymond Norwood Bell, the North Carolina PFC who unwittingly shot and killed Anton Webern a few weeks after the end of World War II. The journal of Robert Walser's sister, Fanny, who took him to the sanitarium where he supposedly committed himself voluntarily—she knew that he would admit to 'hearing voices' and thus inevitably be confined whether he wanted to or not. A confession by Hildegard Panzer, the author of the hoax whereby thousands of dupes in Germany and Argentina (and many neo-Nazis elsewhere) were convinced that Eva Braun and Evita Peron were one and the same person. A well-researched life of Elmer Brick, a celebrity architect, a friend of Gropius and Mies van der Rohe, who at the age of sixty won the Pritzker Prize having never built even one of his vaunted 'humanizations of space.' The tale of Alastair Ross, a longtime chairman of Lehman Brothers, member of the exclusive Knickerbocker and University Clubs of Manhattan, fabulous philanthropist and patron of the arts, father of four children by Ursula Manning, the offspring of one of the city's oldest families, named debutante of the year at her coming out; *and* at the same time, a man with a parallel career as the anonymous and heretofore unidentified author of *The Boom-Boom Saga*, an irreverent and libelously scabrous depiction of the social world in which Alastair Ross was revered, now revealed in his own words to be an unscrupulous gambler drawn to high-stakes poker and faro, a devotee of opium and a major investor in its traffic, lastly a closet queer who participated regularly in New York's well-organized network of orgies, where he went by the name of Sara Lee (Lee being the surname he used in his irregular life—he sometimes referred to himself as 'Nates' Lee, and he relished the company jingle, 'Nobody does it like Sara Lee').

"So that's a sampling of my books, just to give you an idea of what I've done professionally. Which brings me to the possible collaboration between us that I mentioned when we first met. I can tell from the way you and your brother lead your lives that generating publicity is the last thing you want. All the same, your behavior, the rapport between you, is a unique phenomenon that I think deserves serious examination—your superficial similarity, which given your genetic identity is no surprise, and your utter independence from one another, which is a colossal surprise. Clearly this paradox is the consequence of thoughtful choice on your part. How did it come about? How does it work? Why are you both living in this small, out-of-the-way place? I haven't a clue how to answer these questions. I wouldn't dream of speculating about them, and I'm decidedly not interested in the opinions of self-appointed experts. But what I long to see, what I hope and pray I may someday see, is what you and John have to tell us—my dearest hope of all is that you, Paul, will write an account of what has happened. You could do that in any way you choose—you could even use aliases if you had to, anything at all provided there is an autobiography of the two of you—"

At this point Paul, in his agitation, spilled a quantity of ale onto his chinos. Andreas later told Berenice, "He gave me a look so ugly it broke out the sweat on me as though I'd been running. I stared at him and felt I was looking into an abandoned mine shaft."

Paul snapped, "It's out of the question." "OK. I understand. I do, truly, understand. Please, though, try to think of what I said in a simpler form. Think of it as something, just conceivably, not impossible. No more than that, for now—just: not impossible."

"It's impossible." Paul stood up as if to leave. Berenice: "We'll talk about something else. Have some more ale at least, to make up for the spillage."

"No. No, thank you. And thank you for the feast. I'm afraid you've cast your bread before swine."

6

As prologue to their next evening, Geoffrey and Margot had a surprise for their friends. Captain Kipper, the chief of the town's police force, and Sergeant Kerr, whom Geoffrey described as the Captain's right-hand man, had been invited for cocktails so they could meet Berenice and Andreas. With them they observed a notable caution in their conversation, probably a professional reflex. The Captain did his best to play the cut-and-dried officer of no particular age and color (he was a hale forty-five and of a florid complexion), with a vaguely Scottish accent and, in his adopted role, about as emotional as a bagpipe. Berenice quickly detected a softness behind this assumed impersonality. The Sergeant rarely spoke and then usually to support an opinion of his superior's.

These roles were much in evidence when Margot mentioned the "notorious Wicheria," who she'd heard was a friend of the unlikely twins that so fascinated their neighbors. Captain Kipper intervened at once: "The Twins *are* a fascinating subject, but I have to say that Wicheria does not deserve the epithet 'notorious.' She strikes a lively figure in our apparently settled community, but she is a very decent person. I'm sure she'd be happy to tell you what she knows about John and Paul—may I suggest to her that you'd like to meet her? You do agree with me, Sergeant Kerr, that there would be no harm in that?" "Absolutely none, sir," the Sergeant quietly replied. The Captain: "Well then, it's as good as done." Margot and Geoffrey had invited the two policemen for this very purpose; it had been accomplished a little too quickly to bring the meeting to an end. Margot poured another round of whisky, and Andreas obligingly asked Captain Kipper about crime, and his pursuit of crime, in what seemed such a peaceable town. The Captain: "You're right about that, sir—," "Andreas, please." "Very well, Andreas. You're right about that. Isn't he, Sergeant?" "Right on, sir ."

"There are scuffles outside the watering holes on Saturday nights. There is one hopelessly clumsy pickpocket on the loose—we can't lock him up because, first of all, he can't hold his liquor, which is what triggers his thieving urge; so that, second, we always know who's responsible when a bungled pickpocketing is reported; and lastly, his reputable family would go into mourning if they learned of his arrest. So we detain him until he's sober, then send him home. We've never had a murder or a rape (forgive me, ma'am) or even a bank robbery, which is ridiculous—there are three banks in town, all of them sitting ducks. We've lately had new kinds of crime, though: money-laundering and such (our bankers *are* dullards)—I've had to hire an accountant and a former hacker (homegrown, I'm proud to say) to help me with these.

It's a pleasantly quiet assignment, Andreas, I have to admit; somehow I don't think it will lead to significant advancement. What do you think, Sergeant?" "I think, sir, that sooner or later you will be tapped for the position you deserve."

Andreas asked a few more questions; the Captain gave him Wicheria's phone number and email address; the policemen finished their drinks, thanked their host and hostess, and departed. The four friends sat down to dinner, after which Geoffrey proposed to tell his story.

"Like Berenice's, my story concerns a man, one very unlike hers. I met him on a long flight from Sydney to Zurich. The airline was Pan Am, still surviving in the early eighties, after its first rough spell. It had kept its upper deck reserved entirely for business-class passengers, at least those smart enough to request it. It felt like a kind of club. It was there I found myself seated between the spacious aisle and Malachi—Malachi is the name of the 'messenger' who closed the prophetical Canon of the Old Testament. We struck up a conversation that, as often happens between strangers who meet outside their usual circuits, quickly became intimate; and so Malachi told me about his singular life.

"His parents had brought him to Belgium when they left Poland in the early months of 1939, as soon as the Nazis began growling about Danzig—they knew all too well what might happen to them. They made the mistake of settling in Antwerp, where the large Jewish community helped them get started in the diamond trade. Most of its members, together with Malachi's parents, were arrested by the Gestapo and its Belgian auxiliaries during the summer and fall of 1942; they were sent to Dossin, a detention and transportation camp;

the majority of its inmates were shipped off to Auschwitz-Birkenau.

"Malachi had been out shopping for fresh herring at the time of his parents' arrest. He had the sense to take refuge with a Christian family whose sons were friends at public school. Their father helped him obtain identity papers under a new name. To avoid attracting attention by dropping out of school in mid term, he waited until Christmas vacation to leave. The school board certified a medical explanation for his departure.

"He was thirteen years old when he voluntarily began his life as an orphan on the streets. This experience, he told me, taught him all he needed to know about business. He peddled whatever he could find, working the pathetic appeal of his age for all it was worth. His first breakthrough came when he forced his way into a warehouse stocked with jerry cans full of gasoline. He was able to spend six days lugging all he could into a storeroom he'd rented. (He'd wheedled a shopkeeper down to a ridiculously low price: two jerry cans sold paid a month's rent.)

"When the steady increase in the price of gasoline started flattening, Malachi sold his remaining stock and bought a supply of hard-to-find foodstuffs on the black market; and long before truffles, oranges, and corned beef lost their exotic attraction, he had shifted into real estate, renovating abandoned apartments that he sold or rented through the first house-poor postwar years; and thus, success following success, he climbed the hierarchy of profitable commodities. He finally transformed a business in consignment clothing into a brilliant ersatz of high fashion, cornering the trade of

a new class of aspiring women, and this earned him enough
money to pay his way to Canada, a useful step toward gaining
entry to the United States, the mecca of 'hardened entrepre-
neurs' like himself. His plan worked. Two years later he had
reached Boston, which he soon left for the temperate climate
of Miami.

"While still in Antwerp, he had introduced himself to the
reconstituted Jewish community; and he had made many
friends there and, even better, admirers: they heralded his arrival in Toronto with effective recommendations; similar ones
eased his advent in Boston; when he appeared in Miami, he
was wreathed with the honor of having survived the Shoah
and with the prestige of a businessman who had demonstrated how Jewish courage, intelligence, and chutzpah could
overcome dismaying obstacles. The Jewish financial community in Miami welcomed him with a sympathy that Malachi's
wit and youth (he had then just turned twenty-three) transformed into an informal consensus of support. He was provided with an accurate survey of business possibilities where
he might exercise his talents; more remarkably, he was assured
of a guarantee of bank loans that would give him a satisfac-
tory measure of independence in choosing and managing his
ventures. Malachi demonstrated his gratitude by remitting
whatever capital he had saved to the members of the unofficial consortium that was promoting his career; and when the
vouched-for loans came through, he willingly signed promis-
sory notes that bound him to their early repayment.

"However, he did not listen to his benefactors when decid-
ing on his next enterprise. They foresaw him entering new
fields that held a prospect of imaginative development, like

transistors, or ceramic materials for machinery. Instead, Malachi opted for a very conventional business: a Ford concession selling cars and trucks, in the relatively drab community at the edge of Coral Gables, more precisely on the corner of Red Road and 41st Street. The automobile industry's future, already none too promising, was further jeopardized in 1973 by the first oil shock and the mini-recession that followed. Malachi turned this crisis to his advantage, buying the business for less than its lowest estimate. He also justified his decision to his backers with his past record: 'Believe me, I know how to sell. I made a pile hustling so-called pâté de foie gras to Belgians who'd naturally never even heard of it.'

"He showed what he meant with a novel promotional stratagem he invented. He used a second loan to buy a controlling interest in a local TV channel that was about to go out of business. Its programming consisted of regional news, weather forecasts, and extensive reports on neighborhood sports teams; the channel made its small profits from advertisers in Miami-Dade County.

"Malachi programmed an ad for his Ford concession at 9 p.m. on Sunday evenings. It began conventionally enough, with Malachi himself conducting a quick tour of his sales rooms and repair shop, which he'd had minimally spruced up, concluding with a list of his advantageously priced models. At exactly two minutes and thirty seconds into this routine commercial, viewers were without warning or explanation confronted with the opening episode of a serial that they would learn (if they listened carefully) was called *The Medical Wars of Metro-Dade County*. Many viewers surely assumed there had been a technical glitch and would have probably turned off their sets if what they were watching hadn't been so baffling; and those who continued were treated to a second surprise when, after exactly four minutes and fifteen seconds, the episode was abruptly broken off to reveal the malicious face of Malachi smiling out from his array of glistening Fords. He reassured his audience that the story it had been watching would be resumed on the second Sunday of the following month. The first episode would be repeated on the intervening Sundays for viewers hoping to spot clues to the mystery that they'd missed at the first showing. Any spectator too impatient to wait for the next episode would be welcome to pay a visit to the Ford offices at the corner of Red Road and 41st Street during working hours; there Malachi himself would be happy to answer all and any questions.

"Some viewers were puzzled enough to take up Malachi's offer—not many, not right away; but after a few weeks their number passed the hundred mark.

"Malachi had intuitively identified a basic, hard-wired impulse: the desire to resolve the irresolute, to conclude the incomplete, to have the crooked made straight; and (surprise, surprise!) he had located in *syntax* a nexus of this desire as strong as that in melodrama. Malachi knew that where love is not yet fulfilled or disaster looms, a situation can be left dangling at the end of an episode as yet undecided. Logically the worst must happen; but there rises in the viewer an insidious hope that the story will challenge improbability and outwit it. Near the end of the episode that was shown, when a man *leans* forward into the shadows, a narrative voice-over asks, 'Will he place his lips on Mary Ann's expectant mouth? or will he place his foot on the next step of the stairway?' where we have seen that a gunman awaits him and where his curiosity is irresistibly drawing him. The voice continues: 'Dr. Sean now places—' but the film breaks off here. It cuts back to the Ford commercial, where of course there is no hint as to how the sentence will be completed.

"This generated instant, intense frustration. Malachi had discovered that the need to have the sentence completed, no matter how, was as strong as the resolution of psychological suspense. He proved this later, when the serial was in full production: his interruptions then concerned not only questions of love and death but ones like: which ingredient made a gumbo great? or had there been collusion in the choice of hymns and canticles in the services celebrated in Greater Miami that very Sunday? or, the following March, on a special broadcast twenty minutes before the start of the race, who would win the Widener Handicap at Hialeah? 'Why,' a sultry black lady confided after a three-minute-and-six-second tour of Malachi's Ford Plaza, 'Good Counsel, from Darby Dan Farm, Angel Cordero up.' (It helped that the prediction turned out to be right—the winner's odds were significantly shortened, but the canny forecast brought a large contingent of newcomers to Malachi's doors.)

"For the opening episode Malachi had had to work with material and technical help that was readily available: one of the low-grade serials that had come into his possession along with the TV channel, and a sound engineer who added a minimal voice-over track to the sound mix that coordinated the images on the screen with Malachi's needs. Malachi himself supplied the voice: his still-prominent North European accent lent a suitably foreboding tint to his speech.

"Malachi paid careful attention to the diverse elements of his neighborhood, and as his success increased, extended it further and further afield. He was partial to the young—he remembered what it was like to be one of them. He grew his blond hair shoulder-length, until at a judicious moment, he switched to a shaved skull. He sported jeans (tailor-made), Nehru shirts (ditto), and solid black cowboy boots. He liked giving tips on good buys to people his age and if necessary helping them find out ways to meet the price of the cars. He didn't neglect the elderly, who unfailingly reminded him of his dead parents. He knew that many of them were early risers, so he convinced a crazy Hong-Kong-born Chinese-American called Adelaide Lin to lead a tai chi class on the beach twice a week. They loved him for that. He arranged a special rate at Las Delicias de España, the good eatery next door, and sent many of his Cuban visitors there. (In exchange, he requested the use of the restaurant's space for filming occasional scenes of his serial.) He helped finance a Black-Hispanic semipro football team.

"And so it went, with more and more people of all ages and colors crowding into Malachi's concession. Some came for its conviviality. 'Coral Gables Ford' had become 'Malachi's Ford Plaza' after he had purchased an adjoining parking lot. But behind Malachi's secondary ploys lay the essential hook of the fractured serial; and to make that work, to have his clever insight become the irresistible lure that would pull in live bodies, Malachi needed efficient interpreters. (In Antwerp he had hired the best seamstresses in the city to ensure his success in the rag trade.) And here, as he was the first to admit, Malachi was abetted by rare luck.

"One evening during the week that followed the screening of *The Medical Wars of Metro-Dade County*, episode 1, some business friends took him to see a show that many of the local glitterati were touting. You must remember that in the early seventies South Beach showed no inkling of its present glamour. There were perhaps two small hotels, surrounded by boarding houses and modest dwellings to which refugees (mostly Jewish) had been guided by their American brethren. There *was* the beach, however, easily accessible from all parts of the city; and that pleasant setting had been chosen by a company of improvisational performance artists to put on an 'entertainment' every evening at sunset hour. They called themselves The Beach Buoys—a facile name, I suppose, but nothing else about them could be called facile. They were true pros, about twelve regulars—five women and seven men, of which three were gay, three bi, four straight, two undecided; sometimes there would be one or two performers more or less if friends were passing through or regulars went off on temporary gigs. Three of them were veterans of The Second City, most had worked in legitimate theater, in film or on TV, most of them could sing if asked or at least pretend to, one played a creditable tenor sax for dramatic punctuation, another an emphatically sentimental harmonica for mooning and kisses; some were brilliant mimics (but they considered doing celebrity mannerisms a last resort for getting laughs), and every last one was a formidable improviser—they'd sometimes ask for subjects or words from their audience, and off they'd go, not knowing what the others might stick them with but relishing the challenges, ready to give better than they got. They were moderately obscene in performance; off stage, not so moderate.

"Malachi attended the Beach Buoys' show with no more than a polite pretence of curiosity. Ten minutes after its start he knew he'd found fit executants for his project. Their first skit was a reenactment of the original moon walk, accompanied by a deconstructed 'Penny Lane,' with saxophonic riffs on its charming tune and fragments of its lyrics (as Neil Armstrong sets foot on lunar soil, he sings, 'And the fireman rushes in'). Any remaining reservation on Malachi's part vanished when the two astronauts walked into the barber shop as if still moving in a weightless world, a sight both funny and beautiful. At the end of the performance he quickly joined the disbanding troupe: he told them he was so elated by their work that he was inviting them then and there to dinner at a modest but excellent Cuban restaurant in Coral Gables—'superb roast suckling pig, beer, wine, and booze on demand'—where not only would their talents be celebrated but where he planned to make them a proposal they couldn't refuse. He gave them the address of the restaurant, which he called from a nearby phone booth with a request for the imminent arrival of a party of twenty, and be sure to put enough *lechonas* for that number in your capacious ovens.

"Actors seldom refuse a free meal. Malachi had made a favorable impression on most of them, even if some assumed he was some kind of nut. The obviously reputable friends who'd brought Malachi to South Beach (and whom he'd also invited to dinner) vouched for his honesty, his shrewdness, and his bank accounts. When everyone had arrived at Las Delicias de

España and had had time for a drink or two, Malachi stood up and asked for their attention. He presented his promotional plans succinctly and confidently: a routine TV ad for Ford cars and Malachi's Ford Plaza would be interrupted by an unannounced serial, and the serial itself fragmented according to strict application of time slots. With unconcealed pleasure, he expounded his theory of syntactic fracture as a new way of getting viewers involved in a plot, or not even a plot, in a scene, a situation, a character. The Buoys loved these ideas and immediately started thinking up ways to use them. But one of them spotted a problem: 'If it's a serial you're planning, there *has* to be a story. We're not good at telling stories, we're better at sending them up.' Malachi replied, 'I wouldn't think of giving you a story to tell. You make up your own story, or your non-story, or whatever you feel like doing.' He'd define a subject for them, no more than that. Its tentative title was *Medical Warfare in Metro-Dade County*. He'd also supply material to work with, that is, three characters. A white doctor, Sean 'Speedster' Cotton. A black doctor, Johnson 'Hands On' Johnson. A Cuban nurse, Coralina 'Cora! Lina!' Abreu, who was in fact a prestigious *nurse practitioner*, a sexy, savvy freelancer who worked with many doctors, including Speedster and Hands On. (Both of them were after her, but so far neither had made out.) Speedster had his office on Anastasia Avenue in Coral Gables, a block or two from the legendary Biltmore hotel; Hands On worked out of a public clinic in Little Haiti. Speedster drove a stick-shift Mustang, Hands On a F150 Ford pickup (these are the only references in the serial to Malachi's business). Coralina owned a Camry, but only as backup—she had a waiting list of admirers who'd drive wherever she wanted at any time of day or night. Malachi concluded, 'Those are your parameters. What you do with them is up to you.'

"One performer brought up 'a sordid detail: money.' Malachi promptly offered $1,000 a week (worth something like $5,000 these days). That made the Buoys happy: so far they'd been trying out chic variations of passing the hat; it was a comforting windfall to have a regular stipend for doing what they liked for exactly six minutes and fifteen seconds. They all agreed to Malachi's terms; he said he'd have contracts for them by noon the next day. When could they start? 'Yesterday!' So they were in from the beginning, which was two days later, on Sunday evening.

"They did their stuff with gusto; they started innovating immediately. They invented a third possibility for the tantalizing, undecided ending of an episode or incident. Remember the example I gave you a while back? 'Dr. Sean now gambles on sex (good) or death (bad). The Buoys would propose 'places his left pinkie in his right nostril' or 'places ten dollars on Piffle in the third at Hialeah'—that is, neither good nor bad, just undramatic and off the wall.

"So Malachi's clever insight and his choice of interpreters got the job done. After three weeks, the hook had plainly set. A steady stream—a steadily *increasing* stream—of curious fans invaded Malachi's Ford Plaza. His lead actors became objects of street recognition; even the Beach Buoys' beach performances drew bigger audiences once the word had gotten out about their second venue. Malachi managed to always have one or two of them wandering around his showrooms. But Malachi himself soon became the star attraction: as its episodes accumulated, so did the questions about the serial, and he was the only one who could answer them; and if his answers were 'wrong,' that made for even more questions. He was swamped with attention.

"What did Malachi do with all these people? Why, he sold them cars. If customers had any money at all, he would invent credit schedules tailored to their needs and show them how painless it was to become a car owner. He made the brilliant decision to make Mustangs his loss leaders. Ford had stopped producing them in 1970, so Malachi recruited a network of dealers to supply him with second-hand Mustangs. This woke up the entire distribution system. The head office in Dearborn started to take notice of him. He astutely persuaded Carroll Shelby to come to Miami for a weekend, which brought on even more visitors. (Shelby's 1-2-3 win at Le Mans in 1966 had led to the creation of Ford's 'Shelby Mustangs.') It was about this time that Malachi bought the adjacent parking lot and created Malachi's Ford Plaza. Given the guaranteed crowds of potential customers, he was able to sell concessions there at downtown rates. Two years after his first broadcast, he was making enough money to pay off his bank loans *and* buy himself a house at 3810 Alhambra in the elegant green gloom of Coral Gables—as well as his own customized Mustang.

"His business sponsors were proud of him. One way they expressed their affection and approval was to introduce him to the nicest, prettiest, and richest Jewish princesses. To their consternation, Malachi was never interested. He had affairs with women who were original, demanding, and usually married or closely involved with another man. These affairs were not necessarily brief, but they seemed almost planned not to be lasting; they left his friends bemused and the women often embittered. It was the one dark zone in Malachi's Miami life. But he never revealed its source, and few guessed it.

"Malachi didn't give a damn about his success—it was simply a necessary step on the way to satisfying his undeclared, obsessive passion. A passion that he'd kindled and rekindled ever since he'd found himself alone on the streets of Antwerp in December 1942, knowing that his father and mother would never return. He dreamed endlessly of revenging their deaths on what was left of their murderers. And he had imagined a way of doing it.

"Malachi felt nothing but scorn for the legal means of retribution. A former Nazi official was revealed to have served in the administration of a death camp; he was arrested, brought to trial, sentenced to life imprisonment; and soon afterward, given his or her advanced age, transferred to a prison hospital to die a more or less natural death. That was no punishment. He wanted these criminals to suffer as he had suffered after they killed his parents. Of course they had no parents; but many had children, and grandchildren, whom they especially loved to dote on publicly. Killing these children and grandchildren, perhaps torturing them first, might sufficiently devastate the surviving murderers in their last years.

"For a long time Malachi imagined carrying out this project literally. He assembled the family trees of every known or suspected Nazi killer, he located their residences, followed their travels at home and abroad. He researched methods of abduction and concealment, of inflicting pain and death, of recording pain and death, of inconspicuously crossing borders, of disposing of dead bodies....

"As he told me this, Malachi started letting his words tumble out almost uncontrollably; then he paused a long moment as if deliberately returning to a quieter state. In time, he said, he understood that merely initiating his plans required a vast organization of detectives, informers, lawyers, and professional criminals that he could never fund, no matter how much money he made; that it was a scheme that not even the Mossad could have pulled off, although probably one that they themselves had considered. Furthermore Malachi saw that his obsession had begun to contaminate the rest of his life: his loathing of Nazi crimes was slowly spreading so as to include all of Germany, and Germans past and present, and their heirs in every Western country. He knew this was another form of madness, and he had no desire to become a madman. I can't vouch for his exact words, but what he said on the subject, halfway across the Indian Ocean on our flight to Europe, went something like this:

"'So I came to realize that actually killing the children and/ or grandchildren was out of the question. So what, I asked myself, could be the next best step for creating a stink, a stink that served the dictates of my single-minded end? What that necessary end required was a step that would associate a *notional* killing of offspring with the name of the original bastard so that an indelible stink would be glued to him, such that any subsequent step that might cleanse him of it would be out of the question. In which case what was the next step

I should take? Then I remembered what Kafka said about expressing love. A bouquet of roses can't do it. There is only coitus and literature that can achieve this end. Well, if Kafka said so, then choosing literature was my obvious next step (since for "coitus," read "killing," which was not an option). Better than direct denunciation: even if newspapers can still engineer a stink in the right circumstances, nothing can approximate the truly colossal stink that expert writing is capable of, something on the level of Musil or Proust, writing that cuddles up to the so-called truth but never pretends to *be* it, and it was not out of the question that even real names be kept, it was only a lying fiction (that pleonasm!) that made the end, the obliteration of its target as deadly as actually killing it, that is, him or her: all that would be needed as a next step was a hint to e.g., *Der Spiegel*—a prominent member of the media was best equipped to propagate and inflate fictitious shame into a stink of nationwide magnitude: and the subject matter would be of course the killing of the undeserving offspring of each SOB—and if no offspring, the next of kin would do very nicely thank you. But, in the end, that the author of such fictions be an amateur, even an impassioned one, was inconceivable. So not me,' Malachi said: 'my role would simply be dictating the events, step by step, which didn't mean imagination was out of the question, but each step had to be guided toward creating the unique and best effect. I would then not accept anything but the first rate. But in the end I would have the last word. In fact I dreamt of surpassing the initial stink by infusing it with something like a pornographic attraction, so that it would inspire the next potential step, and one or a few readers would kidnap one or a few offspring for an actual killing—now wouldn't that be not only a delicious revenge but a work of genius?'"

Geoffrey stopped. Not another word. Just like that. He was implored to go on. His listeners were all itching with curiosity, he had involved them so slyly in his tale, but he slumped in his chair. At last, all he said was, "I have to wash my face." Berenice and Andreas later confided that they had shared the same impression of watching a well-oiled machine breaking down. It's true that naturally his face was a mess. He'd started crying while he spoke of Malachi's vindictive obsession—it *was* an appalling project, but it was still shocking to see tears running down the face of this normally quiet-spoken man. After a moment he added, "I seem to have painted myself into a corner. I won't be long."

He kept his word and soon came back, very much his "old self"; Andreas later said, "The screws on that leaky sump of his were now bolted tight!" That wasn't quite true. If Geoffrey had fallen silent before without a word of explanation, he now became as communicative as his companions could desire and, what's more, gave them his best reason for being so. His usual urbane composure had surprisingly yielded to a softer, more relaxed liberality.

Geoffrey resumed his story. "To continue from the point I'd reached—that Malachi had decided that his revenge would be accomplished through a work of fiction—what I'd have had to say next is that Malachi wanted *me* to write it. And how could he possibly have thought of me for the job? As far as you know, I'd never written anything. What you don't know is that between the ages of thirteen and twenty-three

I led a totally different life. No one here knows this, not even Margot. Earlier in my conversation with Malachi, for some reason I had told him about it. For some reason! For the same reason we form intimate friendships and initiate rapturous love affairs on skiing vacations and ocean cruises, even on bus rides. Malachi was a likeable, intelligent man, and I knew I'd never lay eyes on him again. It was a golden opportunity to at last divulge my secret, to *someone*. Now it's time to tell it to real friends like you. And most of all to my beloved Margot."

Andreas: "My God, Geoffrey, what were you so ashamed about? Were you a Ponzi schemer? a sly pornographer?" "Oh, shame had nothing to do with it. I changed from one life to a very different other one. The first life became irrelevant. Nevertheless the fact is that for ten years I was a writer. I lived for writing and reading and nothing else. And not any sensible sort of writer, but a poet, no less. I breathed and ate poetry, I planned my present and future around it. I wrote dozens of poems every month, some promising enough to earn the interest of readers I respected. I even published a few in little magazines. Then I gave it up. The details hardly matter. I don't want to dump the whole story on you."

Andreas laughed—a gentle laugh, without a hint of mockery: "No dumping necessary. We're all ears." Geoffrey shook his head. "At least tell us why Malachi really thought he needed a writer—when it came to stories, he was an expert after all." "He said he lacked what I had, what poets had—an irrational passion for pure language, that was what was real for them, and it was essential for him—" Andreas: "But he was right! Geoff, would you consider reciting a poem from your unspeakable past?" To our surprise, he acquiesced.

"It's not one of my best, there's really nothing beautiful in it. But it's relevant to the change in my life. It's my last poem—no, next to last. It's called 'Cassation on a theme by Jacques Dupin.' It was written two months before the May '68 events in Paris—my one prophetic work. Almost every word in it reads like a gloss on what happened then, even the title—one of the first meanings of cassation was 'street music,' and the legal sense was 'quashing,' very appropriate! Jacques Dupin was a well-known poet and authority on Matisse, he was also an excellent boxer, and he used his boxing skills effectively late one afternoon in mid-May when he led an attack on *La Bourse*, the Paris stock market. I have no idea what you think you know about *mai soixante-huit*, but if you weren't there, you don't know anything. I'd been in Paris for a while, studying French poetry at one of the satellites of the Sorbonne. I saw what was happening. I was *part* of what was happening. Just to give one simplistic idea of that: the city I'd left a month earlier functioned according to the social principles of skepticism and discretion, one click away from cynicism and indifference. In the city I returned to, everyone was communicating spontaneously with everyone else, strangers with strangers, old with young, you name it. It was a new world happening over and over. It was a lot more fun than poetry. Let's leave it at that." Andreas: "Not for long I won't!" "You're on. But not now." "What about your poem?"

"It doesn't matter. I quit my poetic studies, took a few courses at HEC, then went back to the States and landed a job as a customs official. That was my revelation. I learned that bureaucracies are designed to kill innovation in the name of predictability; and that the pleasure and purpose of customs offices are to implement rules that are meant to keep things from happening. That meant they were domains ripe for the kind of permanent revolution that I'd glimpsed in Paris during that wondrous month of May.

"One day I spotted in the classified pages of *The Economist* the announcement of a vacancy in the municipal offices of this very town: that of Mercantile Assessor for the Borough. I called the number supplied in the ad to find out what these words meant, and after a lot of prodding deduced it was to run a local board of trade. I sent in my application and to my amazement I was hired for the job. Perhaps I was the only candidate—why would even a moderately ambitious man or woman want to be confined in a place at the end of the world, with no major financial center nearby, no prospects of advancement, and with a job description that sounded like a career's dead end?

"Well, I was full of beans, I had to start my active life somewhere, and so after two final interviews with a New Zealand banker (from Dunedin, of all places) and a municipal representative, who both probably took me for a harmless airhead, I made the journey to this charming town. I stormed into my job with undiplomatic fury, fired three of my staff of four before anyone noticed, and to replace them brought in competent friends from the civilized world with promises of fun and games. I'm told things have improved." Andreas: "Geoff, I learned all about you. You took an office basking in routine and turned it into a dynamo. You 'promoted trade'? You invented the global village! Look what you did for Paul, our recalcitrant twin. I don't think even he realizes how you connected him with his markets overseas." (Berenice thought,

'Kepi Kaps in every pub in Glasgow!') "Maybe. The main thing is, here's where I met Margot." By now she was sitting in his lap with her arms around his neck. Geoffrey: "I know, I know I should have—" "No, it's OK like this. At last I know why you bring all those strange books to read in bed." Andreas surmised: "Ceravolo, Violi, Charles North?" "Yes, also Pastior and Cavalli! You know these people?" "I'm mad about poetry, too. I just can't afford to publish it. We can compare notes, I trust." "You bet. And thanks for getting me out of my chain-mail pajamas. Well, that's my story."

Berenice: "But what about Malachi?" "I declined his proposal as courteously as I could. Naturally, I never saw him again." "Don't you even know his last name?" "It's infuriating. I've forgotten it, and every time I try to remember it, the only thing that turns up is that the proportion of consonants to vowels in his name is 7 to 2—somewhat unusual, but not all *that* unusual, and no help at all in getting his name back." "But you must have taken *some* interest in him." "I emailed him once (at malachi2@gmail.com—I remember *that*). His answer gave me hope he might be slipping out of the stranglehold of his past. He'd let a princess move in with him. But not a Jewish princess—a shiksa! How about that? Now, who goes next?"

7

Geoffrey's question would go unanswered for the next two weeks. Captain Kipper kept his promise to alert Wicheria and did so promptly. She phoned Berenice and Andreas two days after Geoffrey had told the tale of Malachi. She suggested meeting them at the Hunting Horn—"the food's not great but not bad and they have a pretty good combo." Were they free next Saturday? "I'm working nights till then, Sunday I'm meeting friends up the coast. I really want to talk to you about the two boys. My guess is you may have the wrong take on them." Andreas and Berenice agreed to Saturday at 9 p.m.

Andreas had an earlier date that same day: lunch with Geoffrey, who at the Malachi dinner had agreed to explain why he had given up the kingdom of poetry for life in an office. They met at a seafood restaurant reputed for its shellfish chowders and its deep-sea stews. Andreas was as curious as ever about Geoffrey's transformation. At that moment, nothing could have been farther from Geoffrey's mind. As he sat down he was almost giggling with excitement over some new event which, he insisted, he had to tell Andreas about. Andreas: "You as much as promised—" "And I'll keep my promise. But first—" "At least explain one small thing." "If I have to." "What did you mean by 'your chain-mail pajamas'?" "Oh, that! It was a silly kind of portmanteau metaphor, as if not telling my secret was like hiding inside a suit of armor, but it wasn't solid armor just chain mail, and not even a suit, just pajamas. I was only poking fun at myself for being such a ninny, not telling friends like you, not even telling Margot. I thanked you for putting an end to such nonsense. Will that do?" "Sure. So what's got you so agitated today?"

"Do you know Sean Davies?" "The alderman?" "The alderman. As you know, we have no mayor, not officially, and Sean comes closest to being the unofficial one. He's given me lots of support as a saboteur of bureaucratic routine. He asked me to meet him yesterday morning at Willy Aherne's office.

"We happened to arrive at the same time, and before we went in, he pointed out to me an unusual sight. In front of what looked like a private house what you call a doorman was standing, in full doorman regalia, as if he were lording it over the entrance to some grand Fifth Avenue hotel. But the house wasn't even a boarding house, no more than a three-story slim-fronted place that I'd never even noticed. 'Never seen that anywhere,' was Sean's comment.

"Inside Willy's office we found more aldermen. Straight off I saw they were all part of our 'don't wait till it's broke to fix it' clan, as opposed to the partisans of 'let sleeping dogs lie,' our very wet (as you say) antagonists. We were meeting that morning to confirm our majority on the town council for creating an innovation unit in the town government.

"Do you know what an innovation unit is? It's sometimes called an innovation lab, or team, or an incubator, an accelerator, a nudge unit, and so forth. They're all pretty much the same. The best big companies started having them years ago, and now public bodies are starting to use them as well. In most cases a few chosen employees are extracted from their daily grind and told to go out and find ways of renovating the world. I backed the local initiative from the gitgo; Scan and a couple of others came on board pretty soon and as of this morning we're sure of our majority on the council.

"So far so good. But having a majority to vote for an idea is one thing, finding one to raise taxes wouldn't be so easy. We have to look for the money elsewhere, which means borrowing it in the financial markets; theoretically that's feasible but there aren't many precedents, especially in the matter of guarantees—we could hardly use the town's treasury as collateral.

"It was, nevertheless, the town treasurer who intervened in our discussion of possible solutions and ended it: 'I believe I can lead you to someone who will know how to get the money'; and preceding us out of the building, where do you think he carried us but across the street to the place with the doorman! Who, after a few words with the treasurer, let us all inside, where we were taken in by a Warden of the Interior Domain and led into a spacious if rather Spartan office at whose center, standing to greet us with a broad smile and outstretched arms, was a slender gentleman whom I immediately recognized as Michael Bloomberg. His presence in our remote town was known to few of us; he apparently visited it incognito from time to time because he appreciated the pragmatic good sense with which it ran itself. Some of us knew of his enthusiasm for innovation labs—Bloomberg Philanthropies had funded several.

"After an exchange of courtesies and encomiums, Mr. Bloomberg quickly rescued our project from the realm of virtuality by offering, first, to make us a small but significant loan to show that he seriously backed our initiative, and second, to sign an agreement to personally cover the interest on any bank loans our group took out. 'It sounds generous, but I assure you it won't cost me a cent. You'll have my loan to start with, and as well as paying your star researchers to invent the future, you'll start a few very small businesses that generate cash streams—I'll give you specifics another time, things like health kiosks and dating services. Then you'll be able to make the interest payments yourselves, and meanwhile my notorious name will make the banks feel virtuous and safe—that's a bank's definition of happiness. Your worries are over.' And next day—today—when we had breakfasted together, we aldermen went in a body to the bank. To *all three* banks. We didn't want to cause any hard feelings. There were absolutely no hard feelings to be seen. Our bankers insisted we were doing *them* a favor in requesting these Bloomberg-hallowed loans. They offered us more than we wanted, more than we needed. We went out into the world as elated as schoolboys who've been given a surprise half-holiday. Sean is calling a meeting of the whole council next week. We'll wake up those sleeping dogs with a shameless blast. *That's* what happened, dear Andreas, before I met you here. What do you think of 'innovative matrix' as a name for our unit?"

"I do get one point. You're happiest working with people. I'm happy you got what you want and I can't wait to see where you'll go with it. I still can't see why what happened in Paris made you quit writing poetry. You could have had two careers—there was Wallace Stevens/insurance executive, William Carlos Williams/country doctor, and now there's Geoffrey Hyde/trade expediter (or whatever you call yourself)." "But it couldn't work like those others. Here's what happened.

"I came back to Paris about May 10th. I told you how astonished I was. I'd gone to New York a month before hoping to get a first collection of my poems into print. No luck with that. Then after the police occupied the Sorbonne (a sanctuary since the Middle Ages), the student-worker revolt began. The American press as usual got everything wrong—the usual student riots *or* civil war, with De Gaulle as their main target. I didn't yet know what was going on, but I'd been close to people involved in the demos that led up to May to be sure it wasn't what I was reading in the papers. Also I was worried about a cousin, a woman I was very fond of, and when she didn't answer half a dozen phone calls, I went back to Paris, via Brussels with a rental car. (Crossing the French border was a breeze. The immigration officers had joined the general strike, which by then was closing down pretty much the whole country.)

"I arrived on a clear warm spring evening. I was in my apartment eating a picnic supper when repeated explosions began rattling my quiet neighborhood. My friend Sarah Plimpton happened to phone me. She was pleased I was back and quickly realized I had no clue to what was happening. She offered to give me a tour. She arrived a few minutes later, and we walked the two blocks to the Boulevard Saint-Germain, where a seemingly endless crowd of cheerful, mostly young people was proceeding at a lively clip toward (Sarah told me) the Chamber of Deputies. We had slipped into the cortege. Slogans were chanted, by a few at first, quickly taken up by many. A frequent one that night was '*Nous sommes tous des juifs allemands!*,' which Sarah explained (never mind!). At the corner of Rue de Lille everyone came to a halt. The CRS had stopped our progress with so-called 'defensive grenades'— the ones with tear gas. Sarah: 'This happens every day. They watch us building barricades and getting ready to march, and as soon as we start, they charge. Very strange!' Our fellow-marchers' high spirits were not dampened by this failure.

"During the days that followed I rarely noticed *any* sense of failure. For one thing, everybody was having too good a time. Everybody was full of confidence as well. They felt they were winning. After all, they controlled a big part of the Left Bank. The CRS ('Republican' riot police) always pulled back from their tear-gas victories during the night. And whatever happened, people seemed to be learning all the time, taking in new ideas and passing them along as fast as they could. Naturally there were the leftist clichés about class war and solidarity with the unions, but mostly the slogans celebrated individual joy and celebration. Something new had shown up. It was my cousin, Tam, who let me in on the secret. Among the usual competitors for revolutionary authority—dissident communists, Trotskyists, feminists, radical Catholics, anarchists—a movement known as the Situationists, mainly working behind the scenes, had somehow secreted their succulent, subversive vaccines into the mind and soul of this new rebellion.

"The Situationists were best known for their practice of deviation, which meant putting objects or activities to uses for which they hadn't been intended—my favorite example was an American porn film in which all the lines of dialogue had been replaced with maxims from the Little Red Book of chairman Mao. The main target of the movement wasn't late capitalism or neo-fascism, it was hierarchy of any kind. All previous revolutions had overthrown one hierarchy only to replace it with another just as bad and often worse. It wasn't enough to get rid of capitalist hierarchies, *all* social and political hierarchies had to be axed as well. (The PCF, the French communist party, which was run by Stalinists, did not take the Situationists to their bosom.) The only way to make sure this happened was for revolutionary action to become permanent. Direct democracy was the rule of the day, which was perhaps why everybody involved in the May outbreak was having so much fun. If you came up with a great idea, you found you had the power to make things happen, at least until somebody with a better idea came along.

"Here's how I got involved. When I landed in Brussels, I rented a Mini Cooper. Knowing of the gas shortage in France (service stations had shut down as part of the general strike), I filled up the back seat and trunk with seven full jerry cans. Once I'd settled into life in Paris—one or two demos were enough to make me want to join the party (and I don't mean the PCF!)—I wondered what kind of a contribution I could make. It would have to be inconspicuous; foreigners caught tossing paving stones were bundled out of the country within hours. Perhaps my little car and a respectable supply of gas might be useful. One morning I went to the Censier branch of the Sorbonne to offer my services—that's where the student-workers action committee was headquartered.

"When I walked into the main building I was treated to a surprise. The high walls of the entrance hall had been painted from floor to ceiling with blackboard paint. Lines of text had been chalked over the entire surface. They were full of new ideas for the 'ongoing revolution' and instructions for applying them. The language was elegant and sharp. I took out my little camera hoping to record some of it. I was promptly stopped by a young man nearby: no photographs. I told him these perishable sentences were too good to lose. He said he understood, but what was written on the walls wasn't meant for the ages, it was meant for today and today only. True enough—when I came back the next day, all the words I'd seen had been erased and new ones equally inspiring had taken their place. I felt a slightly horrified respect for the volunteers who'd given up a night's sleep to get this work done. That was Situationism in action.

"The student-workers committee asked me to drive a couple of their members to factories a hundred kilometers or so from Paris. These were places where no reliable information about the uprising was available. I made five of these trips over the next ten days. We had only a few hours at our destinations to spread the good word, not enough to have had much effect—the 'unions' in these factories were usually set up by management, with in-house security systems to get rid of troublemakers. But what happened in the car on the way out and back almost made up for our disappointments. I traveled with three new passengers each time; invariably one of the three, while full of enthusiasm for our cause, would be stuck in some dumb hang-up that he'd be better off without. On the drive out, the remaining three of us would give our victim free rein to develop his nasty foolishness, so we were well prepared to bludgeon it to death on the way home. The roadsides of several *autoroutes* were littered with the corpses of homophobia, machismo, family values, and racism (mainly toward Arabs) that our happy fools at last metaphorically chucked out the window, and the four of us would drive into the weirdly carless streets of the metropolis singing the passably irrelevant stanzas of *L'Internationale.*

"On the last of these excursions it was my turn. I should have known something was up. Two of my three passengers had been with me on earlier trips, a practice not forbidden—'prohibiting is prohibited!' was a conspicuous slogan—but not encouraged either. On the outward leg I was suckered into relating my love affair with poetry in preposterous detail; no sooner had the drive back begun than my ordeal began as well. My passengers started needling me rather gently, and they were never less than affectionate, but soon they were pitching it in red hot; for a while I tried dutifully to stick it out, but I was gradually and meticulously divested of my addiction. I was made to see where it was leading me: a place where poetry would be a refuge, a line of defense to keep me safe from the active world—that world being then an obviously threatening one. I had no use for politically committed poetry—revealing injustice is better done with prose. I knew that one way poetry could be revolutionary was by subverting the conventions of language, by addling its normative expectations, by showing that words were almost never saying what they claimed to be saying. Could I have followed that path? Maybe. On that car ride my one-time friends showed me ... they reminded me of a Situationist tag: most of us were like people in prison who kept going through days of confinement by remembering moments of being free and imagining future moments of freedom, and as a poet, I remembered past moments of ecstasy and imagined future ones, but like the prisoner I was, I was limited to surviving my present condition.

"*And* I'd learned another way of using language. After a few days in May I knew how to talk to men and women, how to wake up their dormant possibilities—I could 'manage' them, not by psychological manipulation but by provoking them into moving on.

"When most people talk about May 1968, they say its political and social effects were disastrous. It's true that an uprising launched to defend the independence of the university in the end destroyed its authority. It's true that many activists ended up in cushy jobs under Mitterand. It's true that many others less fortunate drifted into poverty or bitterly gave up their progressive ideals. That was especially true of those from the middle class. They felt they had to create valid identities for themselves, they went to work in factories or started communal farms. Those people missed the point.

"What was great in the best days of May was the exuberance not only of direct democracy but of *winning*. We brought about the longest general strike *ever* in an advanced economy. We had the government wetting its collective pants. Cabinet members were renting apartments in Brussels to escape imminent disaster. De Gaulle went off secretly to beg the army not to desert him. We were on a roll, not for long, just a few days. Not then or afterwards did I ever think about having a valid identity, it was never a concern for those of us who didn't want to lose what we'd experienced. As a poet on the fringe I'd learned enough about being 'downtrodden' not to have to wreck myself running a machine!

"For some of us there was a good way out: keep on changing life and lives by starting with our own. To someone like me who'd been addicted to Freud this was obvious. Just as it was obvious that you can't change people by bashing them with good ideas. (Shaw said, 'Reformers have the idea that change can be achieved by brute sanity.') Women understand this better than men. They see that politics begins in participation, in socialization, they're easily committed to what one of them called 'a critical renewal of everyday life.' Me too—when I met Margot, who'd been through rough times as a belligerent feminist in Seattle, she took to me partly because I was no dogmatic leftist but a pragmatic, day-to-day saboteur.

"Listen, that's the best I can do."

Andreas: "I wish I'd been there." It was an honest remark; but Andreas still couldn't understand why his friend stopped writing poetry. Geoffrey's enthusiasm for the innovative lab showed that acting directly on the way people function brought him a meatier satisfaction than the slow, indirect notation of poetic thought; but what of the slow, indirect side of him, where strange sights and sounds coalesce out of nothing, or nothing more than the caressing or crashing encounters of words aspiring to be pure as music, as mesmerizing as the sky on a cloudless night?

Andreas had time to go home and have a refreshing nap.

With Berenice he then went back into town to keep their appointment at the Hunting Horn with Wicheria.

She was waiting at the bar. She waved to them as they walked in, as if there could be any doubt that she was the one they were looking for. Berenice immediately allowed herself the pleasure of detailing her appearance: high-heeled black patent-leather sandals; a flounced red taffeta skirt, half-calf length; a broad belt of green snake skin; a loose muslin blouse of softer red; on her arms silver bracelets that slid and clinked when she moved; no rings; red-currant pendants on her ears; long thick auburn hair, with an occasional curl (not smoldering red as reported). When she stood up and walked smiling toward them they felt nothing so much as a pleasure in being alive, which Wicheria seemed to confirm with her first words, "The Captain told me you were the hottest couple in town."

Knowing there would be much talking in store, she had secured a relatively quiet corner table for them. At Wicheria's suggestion, they ordered plain fare and good wine. She quickly brought up the subject of the twins and asked Berenice and Andreas how they had become interested in them and what they'd learned about them since they'd arrived in town. The couple answered her questions concisely and cheerfully, not hiding their disappointment at their dinner with Paul.

Wicheria: "Paul couldn't possibly accept your offer as 'not impossible.' There's no way he could even *dream* of saying yes to it. That's not only because he has a thorny side.

"This is what I think. The two of them are playing *one* game, the same game. Or putting on one and the same act. One act with two sides to it. Or two actors—for instance: one sort of sweet, one sort of tough, sweet John, tough Paul, John gets affection, Paul gets respect, together they get both. Or at least that's their plan. I said this is what I think, but I bet you nobody in this place knows them like I do. I have to tell you one other thing. I never talk about Paul to John or John to Paul. And if I did—and if Andreas you did—it's not John or Paul who could tell you what's going down between them, only the two of them could do it. I'm not even sure if they sat down one day and laid out the rules, or the thing just evolved, seeing what worked and what didn't. No matter how they set the game up, they had it down perfect when they moved here, arriving on separate dates, going straight to separate lodgings, drinking in different neighborhoods. Just managing the logistics proves they'd planned it together. You know they've never even been seen in the same space, not *ever*. Although there've been quite a few almosts."

Andreas: "But what's the point? What do they get out of it?" "Whatever they get they get it as a pair. I'm totally sure each of them knows what the other's been up to." Berenice: "What makes you so sure?" "Lots of wiseacres make a point of telling each twin 'what he may not have heard.' Then when I talk to either of them he'll say that he knows these things already—'Oh, you should ask my brother John about that' or 'That's Paul's department.'" Berenice: "You mean they communicate?" "It sure looks that way." "But how?" "I dunno. Invisible ink? Encryption? I long to get a look inside their Macs, but I almost never get a chance. They both always insist on my place." Andreas: "What's that mean?"

Wicheria: "Are you up for a confession? Real intimate?" The couple made it clear they were. "OK. I've had affairs with both of them. I'm *having* affairs with both of them. *Very* laid back. No strings, no expectations. I love going to bed with them, they're different but each fun in his own way. Mostly they're true to form—gentle John likes to make things last forever, steely Paul comes on like a bullet train. Now hear this: Paul likes (read: insists on) making love with the lights out, and I don't mean down: *out*. And why? He doesn't want me to see his body, he's so shy. Sweetie-pie John has to have all the lights on so he can be sure of seeing *my* body, otherwise he can't make it. It's fine by me either way, but it's not behavior I'd have expected. To get back to my point: what they've done is combine their similarities—what twins are supposed to have—with absolutely separate ways of living. Taking them together, that makes for a whole, or maybe not a whole but a very full life, here in this one place and time. That way it makes *some* kind of sense—not just in my bed, either."

Berenice: "At least it's conceivable. I'll have to think about it." Andreas: "Me, too. In the meantime, since you've been so frank about yourself, Wicheria—" "People also call me Witchy, for speed—" "OK, Witchy, could you tell us more about how you became the way you are, how you came here, for instance, how you learned to be so 'laid back' about sex at only, what are you, twenty-one, twenty-two?" "Close. Plus one." "So?" "You don't want to hear my whole story." Berenice: "Oh yes, we do. We're *very* into stories, life stories especially, you have no idea." "That's pretty weird. OK. My relaxed attitude about sex was the direct outcome of my tragic childhood."

They were then regaled with their first hearing of Wicheria's laugh—bass clarinet to clarinet to softened high flute. She then shook her head, rather solemnly. "It may not have been tragic, I'm not sure what 'tragic' means, but it was sad enough. Still, as you must have noticed, I recovered. My last name is Bentwick—maybe five people here know that, and four of them are town clerks. Maybe for starters I should talk about the Bentwick dynasty. It's not irrelevant, it was relevant from the start, as you'll see.

"The start means Paul Bentwick, born in 1830 in Maastricht into a family of money changers.

"He was my great-great-grandfather. He left Holland at the age of seventeen after first 'lightening his father's overburdened hoard' of one hundred pounds sterling. He sailed to New Zealand where he invested his cash in a flock of eight hundred sheep. He managed his investment so well that ten years later the flock numbered over thirty-eight thousand. Over those years he made what he called 'retail' sales to cover his expenses (grazing rights in those days cost a few pennies an acre). These sales were yearly offloadings strictly kept to a running average of 5 percent of the steadily growing flock. That came to about eight thousand animals in the ten years. He sold his holdings in 1857 for close to half a million pounds and arrived in America soon afterwards. He settled first in northern New England, then in Boston, finally New York City.

"You may be wondering how I know all this. If you're a Bentwick child, you get it drilled into you before you learn how to read. On Christmas Eve each of us was given a quiz on family history; if you failed, no presents.

"Paul Bentwick kept up his New Zealand connections. He was a friend of Samuel Butler's, who made his fortune the way Paul had, and he was one of the consortium that bought up the land we're living on. Also the tracts of hinterland beyond.

And that superintended the creation of our nifty little town."
(Andreas: "New Bentwick! At last I know why.")

"In 1859 Paul married Mary Gifford, the daughter of an old whaling family he'd frequented with his family on a summer vacation in Fairhaven, Massachussetts. The following year they had a son, the first John Bentwick, my great-grandfather. In 1862 Mary's sister, Abbie, married Henry H. Rogers. Henry was on his way to becoming a key man in John D. Rockefeller's fabulous development of Standard Oil. The two families had remained close. In early 1881, John Bentwick was about to turn twenty-one. In homage to his majority, Henry Rogers told him in strictest confidence that Rockefeller was about to launch a new corporate entity: the Standard Oil Trust. John's parents had for the same occasion allotted him a decent sum; on the day that Standard Oil Trust made its public offering on the New York Stock Exchange, John bought five thousand shares. It proved to be the inside tip of all times. For once the expression 'an embarrassment of riches' rang true; John was soon spreading his bonanza to others, publicly and privately.

"So his son, my grandfather, the second John Bentwick, born in 1903, had a substantial stake with which to play financial games. They were something he enjoyed and was fairly adept at. He inherited his father's seat on the Stock Exchange—a position that gave him privileged access to information, incoming and outgoing. During the fall of 1929 he got wind of a spate of urgent messages from the Parisian headquarters of the Banque Saint-Phalle to its American branch. These messages contained increasingly emphatic instructions to sell all of its holdings on the New York Exchange without delay. The last of these messages was delivered on the

Thursday preceding Black Tuesday; like the previous ones, it was ignored by the American Saint-Phalle directors.

"It was not ignored by John Bentwick. He had independently researched the few leads provided by the French bank and come to the conclusion that their decision was justified. In the few days between making his own heretical choice and the disaster of October 29, he liquidated the totality of the Bentwick family investments, buying government bonds in their place. The operation could not be effected without informing all the Bentwicks concerned. At a family conclave in his New York house on a Saturday evening, an animated discussion climaxed in a proposal to have my grandfather confined to a lunatic asylum. But by the following Wednesday his vindication had already begun.

"My father, Duff Bentwick, born in 1942, took little interest in business matters. But even he managed to make his contribution to the Bentwicks' wealth. When André Malraux was indicted for stealing Khmer art at Angkor Wat in the 1930s, Malraux managed to sequester a considerable part of his sculptures with a partner. This partner later died without indicating their whereabouts. Traveling in Europe after World War II, Duff Bentwick came across this trove in the storeroom of an Italian dealer who had no idea of their nature. Duff managed to buy them for a minute fraction of their value. He then set them aside for several years to 'decant,' as he put it, meaning to lose all trace of their provenance. He finally sold them in the early fifties and made his own small fortune. But his story doesn't end there.

"Duff's older brother, the third John Bentwick and present heir, was born in 1940. This John is alive and flourishing.

He claims, with some justice, to be first and foremost a philanthropist. 'Someone,' he says, 'has to repay society for my forbears' ill-gotten gains.' He can't resist adding, 'To which I contribute my share. Whenever I give a million dollars to a noble cause, its sponsors shower me with invaluable tips. My insider trading hasn't just paid for your schools and doctors. It's paid for every damn pair of those crazy shoes you love to buy.'

"You see, John has been my guardian since I turned fifteen.

"My mother died of leukemia when I was nine. Duff and I were bereft. Each of us in a way that was of no help to the other. When he looked at me, he saw her. When I looked at him, I saw not-her. Was there no love between us? Maybe, but we didn't have the right vocabularies for it. I screamed at him. The screams meant, why are you alive and not her? His response was pale silent faces, which could have meant, I agree with you. She'd been beautiful and tender. He was beautiful, too; he got colder by the day. He'd long before been made a major in the US Army reserve. When we invaded Iraq, he'd finagled and operated and maybe even bribed some fellow officer to be recalled to active duty, in spite of his age.

"The Bentwicks ganged up on him in horror, to no avail. He was killed in the second battle of Falluja, in 2004, by a roadside bomb. His friends and relatives went wild asking why? why? I knew why. So did the third John Bentwick. So did Duff: he wanted out. His beautiful tender wife had deserted him. His shrew of a daughter hated him. He got what he wanted. He asked John Bentwick to take care of me.

"John was up for that. But it took him two years to become my guardian. John had a bum reputation in some quarters.

He'd never married. He was conspicuously not gay. But he'd had numerous affairs, some of them notorious. That means with newsworthy married women. At sixty-four he showed no sign of slowing down. He'd never held a job where his responsibility had been tested. His philanthropy didn't count for much—'with his money, it's the least he can do.' His backing of legitimate causes, like the right to free speech for *everybody*, made him an easy target: he was defending neo-Nazis, racists, and other sickies. Putting an adolescent girl in the hands of such a man was unwise.

"My father had packed me away in a prestigious Protestant boarding school when he went off to war. My teachers, the headmaster, even a few of its trustees all thought I was such a great student and human being that I should be left to their care. I should definitely not be confided to a dissolute millionaire. The dissolute millionaire by the way had been paying for my schooling and all my living expenses since my father died. There was no objection to that, naturally. Also naturally, nobody asked the girl at issue what *she* wanted.

"Actually I might have been pretty confused about what to answer. I hadn't yet seen that much of John. But the other Bentwicks rallied round. They convinced the world that being adopted by John Bentwick would be any child's dream. At worst he'd make her life a grand party. He'd certainly never corrupt her, and if he tried, the Bentwicks would be on him like a pack of bloodhounds. Practically every adult family member called on the representatives of the guardian ad litem until they convinced them of John Bentwick's honorableness. The family court judge only had to add his seal of approval. So the Bentwick family put an end to public debate about me. On my fifteenth birthday I became the ward of my uncle.

"This prospective patron, this bachelor in the prime of life, proved a gentleman in the grandest sense, such a figure as never (except in a dream or an old-fashioned movie) would have risen before a flustered, anxious girl out of New Hampshire. Where I was concerned, he was an absolute dreamboat. He didn't pack me off to another school but had me tutored by young men who were as smart as can be and usually cute. He took me out on dates with his lady friends. They were usually ten or fifteen years younger than he was, and they were pretty cute too. He got them to teach me about life. They liked doing that—for one thing I *really* listened. I heard a different version of the world from the one I'd been told at my oh-so-pious school. I think that's what John was after; that's how I started becoming 'laid back' about sex. (Did I really say that?)

"My John took me everywhere he could—that meant lots of places. He's what they used to call a dilettante. He played the flute so well professional chamber musicians invited him to record with them. He was such a good freehand draughtsman, he could entertain a picnic's worth of kids sketching their portraits. He was an honorable tennis player. (He had no use for golf, 'although the cruising isn't bad,' he confessed.) He loved classical ballet. He'd never taken lessons so he made damn sure I did. That was hard, but at least it wasn't lacrosse. When he 'took possession of me,' as he liked to say—incidentally he never made a hint of a pass at me, which sort of pissed me off, since I was mad about him and at eighteen not exactly repulsive—I had turned fifteen. He was living in Boston, and I thought that's where we would live. But it was to his county home—an old family place in Chatham, on Cape Cod—that he wished us to proceed.

"I soon learned why. He'd turned it into a refuge for eccentric Bentwicks. Actually there wasn't any such thing. The Bentwick family was almost a hothouse of eccentricity. Still, some of the residents at Chatham were out on the edge— two unmarried teen-age mothers, two serious alchemists, a fanatic who dedicated his exceptional wits to devising a sure-fire system for playing the horses. (He finally succeeded. The trouble was, his system allowed on average only one chance a month to place a bet—'Too boring!' he concluded.) There were also more predictable characters: two poets, one composer, and one graphic artist, all of whom John considered promising but were too eccentric for any school. All of them were cheerful and seemed to enjoy their privileged freedom. They threw frequent parties that lasted late, where I got to hear all the new groups. They gave me books to read that made my hinges pop.

"Of course I wasn't there all the time. John kept taking me off to gallery openings and dance recitals in New York (and my first opera: *Lulu*!) and concerts in Boston and Cambridge. On one trip I had my first liaison—I'm almost certain John set it up, but I didn't dare ask him. Anyway it was a good start. I must have been seventeen.

"Meanwhile I became a super brilliant student. I scored so high on my SATs I got full scholarship offers from all the best places. I visited a couple of them and was not turned on. John had been full of praise for my scores; but I think he was relieved when I said no thanks to the Ivy League. He said I was learning enough from his renegade cousins and his ambitious tutors. I hope he's right. I can still take down ace deconstructionists and discuss variations in the cosmic microwave background with any passing cosmologist! And then John took me on longer trips. He'd introduce me to makers and shakers he admired, economists in Chicago, architects in California. I kept learning from all of them. They'd talk to me as soon as they saw I wasn't another cute chick.

"The strangest trip of all was to Miami. John knew a businessman there he thought was a real original. He wanted him to move to New Bentwick, yes here, it would be right for him and he for it. He said to me, 'You keep saying you owe me so much. You say you want to pay me back. So here's your chance.' 'Huh?' I said. 'I'll introduce you. You get into his life any way you want. You overwhelm him—yes, you can. You can take him over. Then you can bring him to New Bentwick to your Uncle John.' 'You're asking me to fuck somebody I haven't even seen?' 'Absolutely not. He'll be eighty years old next year. Good Lord, I thought you'd never get around to using that word in front of me.' 'So what else can I do?' 'Dazzle him out of his wits! You're asking *me*? You talk shop with astrophysicists, maybe you can teach him gin rummy.' 'You know that for you—' 'Yes. And I'm asking you. His name is Schlemkes.'"

"Wait," Andreas interrupted. "Can you spell that?" Wicheria obliged. Andreas counted the letters. "Seven consonants, two vowels. Like the name Geoffrey couldn't remember. Is his first name Malachi?" Wicheria: "Don't tell me you know him?" "No. But our friend Geoffrey Hyde does. You mean to say you're the beautiful shiksa that moved in with him?" "Moved in, no. But I hung out at his place all the time." "I thought he'd fallen for—" "He did, in a way. We really clicked.

You know he's been hung up on this Jewish revenge shtik. I started getting him to see he was looking the wrong way, timewise. He's still got great ideas in him." "You should inform him that the man who sat next to him on a Pan Am flight from Sydney to Zurich in 1980 (I think), the one he wanted to hire to write his book, is living in New Bentwick and is starting up an innovation—"

The conversation could go no further. The four-piece band that had drawn out a few hesitant dancers with "La Vie en rose" now broke into the snappier "Winchester Cathedral," at whose first chords Wicheria grabbed a startled Andreas by the hand and pulled him toward the dance floor.

The vocalist was getting the song right—sad words juggled by happy music:

> Winchester Cathedral
> You're bringing me down
> You stood and you watched as
> My baby left town.

Andreas was protesting, "But I can't dance to this stuff!" Wicheria: "You will." *She* certainly could (but she kept her first turns small to let her partner get started). He was timidly shifting from foot to foot. She was moving a shoulder or a foot or her head or hips in no recognizable order. He tried repeating one of her movements—"You're doing steps, Andreas baby, never do steps. Just listen to the music." (Andreas reported all this to Berenice later.) "OK. Imagine your left hip is a fixed point in space and around it the rest of you can do anything, *anything*." She demonstrated.

"Fine, you can do what I do but just once! Then you make up your own moves." Not knowing what to do, Andreas started loosening bits of his frame, wiggling for instance. Meanwhile, to calls from the sidelines of "Go for it, Witchy!" the lady put on a show—graceful slides, spins, and leaps that set her loose bright clothes and her long hair swirling about her in savvy escalation to an apex at the end of the song— "My baby left town" repeated over the electronic din of two guitars, a double bass, an agitation of drums—an apex with Wicheria's right leg raised high behind her in a classical arabesque. Berenice watching prayed her Andreas remembered enough from his ballet evenings to do what he should; and he did, dropping to his right knee and taking her waist in his two hands to support her arabesque now *penché*, her raised leg perfectly vertical, sheathed to the slight parenthesis of her underbutt in glittering-green, irregularly see-through pantyhose, held straight and pointed for five full seconds until the two dancers broke into giggles, stood up and kissed each other on the cheek, the onlookers cheered away, and Wicheria led Andreas back to our table—a happy, slightly reconditioned Andreas, and still all mine!

8

M ine?"
      After our lunch with John, when it became certain
that neither of the twins would ever publicly tell their story, I
decided to preserve these pages that I began writing months
ago, the day after I met Andreas. They are not meant to replace what Andreas hoped to publish. They are no more than
a chronology of our life here, a kind of journal that has now
unexpectedly changed into a memoir. Now Berenice can say
"me," "we," and "mine." And Berenice's new name is "I."

   We finally met John at the same spruce and pleasant bar
where he'd long ago happily accosted me. Its name is the
Bentwick Arms; it serves light lunches as well as drinks, including the Sardinian vermentino that Andreas had been
longing to taste ever since I'd mentioned it to him.

   John was visibly pleased to see us. He looked hale and
happy; his head and forearms were bronzed from his hours
at sea; he smelled of salt and fresh fish. For no reason, but
with childlike glee, he told us about his latest excursion early

that same morning: setting out in black night by the light of whale-oil lamps, coasting through billows of fog that only thinned an hour after the first daylight had filtered through their woolly gloom, by which time the crew had pulled up their first fine-meshed nets, Captain Edwin Donnelly having known exactly where they were ("Squid Cavern thirty foot to starboard"), "we brought up many pounds of scarlet shrimp and poddernails, enough to fill the live-well.

"When the fog lifted and we were basking in a warm November sun boosted by a mild breeze from the sea, we spied a congress of gulls romping above a patch of whitened water a quarter mile to the north. Captain Donnelly cried out as if at market, 'Mackerel, morwong, and fine john dory!' We headed straight that way, and he was soon proved right. We had two nets out behind us and netted more than eight hundred pounds of those same fish, with a few dozen hake and blue moki among them. We made three long passes—the Captain complimented me on the spiral paths I took, which added greatly to my joy. The value of the catch was heightened by the abundance of terakihi among the morwong, a favorite for grilling in these parts, and by the great number of john dory, a fish prized in many lands. Our two lesser 'mates' joined in the excitement. (A good haul would fatten their day's wage. We call them mates to give them a smidgeon of dignity, but in truth they are deck hands. I'm the only one the Captain trusts with the handling of our craft.)

"Once we'd iced down our harvest it was still early morning; we chose to venture into deeper waters—perhaps a mistake, we spent two barren hours offshore where the breeze was more a cold, ruffling wind, and the two long lines we'd put out took not a single strike until, now feeling resigned and with our earlier elation souring, we turned homeward. And then our discontent was scattered: we hauled in two albacore, each close to a hundred choice pounds. Having no more ice, we secured them under water to the sides of our boat to keep them fresh. The Captain stood aft with his .30 caliber rifle in hand lest predators should appear; none did. So we came to port a happy crew again. Pale ale never tasted so good as the first stoup I drank here before you came in. And you, Andreas, what do you think of the vermentino?"

"The best!" Andreas dreaded spoiling John's sunny mood; but the subject he was afraid would exasperate him was the one that had prompted this meeting. He deployed prodigies of tact in retelling the same story that had so disastrously affected Paul, emphasizing his seriousness as a publisher; emphasizing the seriousness of his interest in the tale of two brothers who had organized their lives with such efficient originality; performing miracles of narrative evasion to avoid mentioning Paul by name, until at last he had to: "I asked Paul if he would write your story. He refused."

"I gathered as much." John's face was quickly shadowed with melancholy. Andreas knew better than to try and restore its cheerfulness; he made the plunge: "John, please tell the story yourself—the story of both of you. It deserves to be told. Unless you do it, some journalist, or maybe an academic, will disassemble the facts and rearrange them in a chic or respectable interpretation and call that your story. It's bound to be a travesty of your lives. Only you can say what really happened." (But Andreas later told me that even as he spoke these words, he thought: But there *is* Wicheria!)

John: "I can't." I asked him, "Can't because you don't want to? Or maybe it frightens you?"

"Why should it frighten me? There's nothing shameful about it. As for wanting or not wanting, that's irrelevant. I don't even know what to think about that."

Andreas: "But it would come to matter inevitably."

"Perhaps. But when I said 'I can't,' I meant that I'm bound not to. Paul and I have a sworn agreement not to discuss one another in public, certainly not in print. I suppose that right now I'm technically breaking my promise. But you are clearly good people, I hope we'll become friends, the three of us. I feel that you deserve a few words of explanation. But very few.

"It was precisely because we knew how odd our behavior appeared to outsiders—all the more so in a community as small as this—that we came to our agreement. I think it's worked rather well. Many people wonder; and most of them are discreet, they let us live our lives as we wish. We have friends enough, but I'd say we're accepted with respect rather than affection. Although Captain Donnelly I think has taken me to his heart."

Andreas: "Do you think that it was your pact that made Paul turn me down? He did so very angrily."

"I don't know. And if I did know, I wouldn't tell you! You see, our arrangement is an outcome of events long past. It's a way of being able to live near one another without having our earlier history lead to discord or even disagreement of any kind. I can't speak for Paul's respect for our bargain, but as for myself, I shall never break faith with it. As I hope you can tell, I say this without a jot of anger."

I gave his nearby hand a reassuring squeeze; Andreas said,

"None that my tetchy nerves can detect. I'm not surprised by
your saying no. I suppose I shouldn't have asked you at all. I
usually feel very strongly about putting questions. It reminds
me too much of the day of judgment. You start a question and
it's like starting a stone—the stone starts another stone, and
soon there's an avalanche. If you'd said yes, you'd have con-
demned yourself to a firestorm of inner violence—I think!
But I *am* disappointed. Among all my ventures in implausible
lives, yours would have been the crown jewel. If *you* had told it.

"Now no more about that, not ever. I'd like to raise another
question, one that can't possibly threaten your peace of mind
and that's often mystified me: What brought you and your
brother to New Bentwick?"

"That *is* easy to answer.

"The first item was an article in the *National Geographic*—
you probably know it, the American travel magazine, Berenice certainly does. The article listed the town as a place
worth a visit by curious travelers; it provided a short history
partly to explain why it was interesting. It was discovered (so
we learned) around 1875 by the writer Samuel Butler, who
spoke or wrote about it to a number of very rich capitalists,
of the enlightened variety, I guess one would say. It was just
a village then, called something like Onipouri, mainly fishermen and a few artisans.

"It was already a special sort of place, in its small way—
for instance, the fishermen practiced what we'd call sustain-
able fishing, not only inshore but over a rather vast tract of
ocean surrounding their bay. They'd somehow figured out
that if they caught too many desirable fish, there wouldn't be
enough around for the next generation, so they laid down

limits to the seasonal catch of john dory, albacore, and hake, as well as shellfish such as crayfish, *pāua*, scallops, and crabs. The village already exported much of its production to the south island, at first smoked or dried, and later, once they'd installed the necessary equipment, frozen, at that point extending their market to virtually the entire Commonwealth.

"The village fishermen didn't impose their limits only on locals but on any outsiders who visited the waters the New Bentwickers laid claim to. They even had a fleet of little gunboats to make sure no intruders left with more than their paid-up allotment of fish. Remember that at that time laissez faire capitalism was encouraged in many lands and initiatives tolerated that would be prohibited today.

"The enlightened capitalists in any case were impressed by these practices as well as by a kind of pragmatic optimism in the village's approach to public affairs. They formed a consortium and made a deal with its residents. The capitalists would build the first indispensable additions to the village; they would control the distribution of land and the design of the new town, and this right would pass to the successors that they designated. In exchange they would endow in perpetuity the possessions and activities of the present population, with the right to sell, rent, and bequeath them to whomever they chose, on condition that the said sales, rents, and bequests never alter the uses, nature, or functions of their possessions and livelihoods. Fishermen could continue to fish and cobblers to cobble, but they could not dispose of their properties or rights to the benefit of new enterprises. That didn't mean much in the 1870s, but now it means no casinos, no grand hotels, no high rises.

"And nobody's complaining. You see the first capitalists were far wealthier than what was required for their first commitments to New Bentwick, the point being that they had a good chance of maintaining and increasing their policy of endowment and support either through their children, if any were interested, or through legacies to eligible young outsiders. Until well into the twentieth century, remember, there was no inheritance tax and virtually no income tax to limit their investments.

"It's astonishing how continuously the original policy has exerted its effect—look at John Bentwick, Wicheria's guardian, he's the great-grandson of one of the town's founders and still promoting the place. That first generation bought all the village land for a generous price, and it also bought and incorporated thirty-three thousand acres of hinterland so that the town could become as self-sufficient in meat, bread, and produce as it already was in fish. They and their successors created little businesses—a ship chandlery, a clothing store, an outlet for farm equipment, a pharmacy-*cum*-infirmary, the little lodging houses and eateries; they recruited qualified craftsmen to satisfy the town's growing needs; they helped fund the first newspaper; they invited three Christian denominations to build churches (chapels, really) and even Persians to open a mosque and a Bahai temple, and Jews to provide a synagogue; they helped these sects establish schools, and they saw to the building of secular primary and secondary schools, topping up salaries sufficiently to lure good teachers from their customary paths.

"As the project gained in renown, it added to New Bentwick's attractiveness, not only to teachers but to writers and artists, even to business people unconventionally inclined. The undeclared rule that the community would be English-speaking didn't make for provinciality. From the start its directors used it to seek out immigrants not only from Britain and the United States but Australia, Canada, the Raj, Britains's African colonies, and of course New Zealand—a vast international reservoir of human material.

"Word kept spreading that this little community was developing according to unspoken principles that might be encapsulated in two words: what works. (However, any applicant for residency or employment who as much as whispered the word 'Utopian' was rejected out of hand.)

"After we had read the *National Geographic* article, Paul and I did a little more research, all of it encouraging. We ended having a meeting at the New Zealand consulate in London with someone from New Bentwick itself. She told us that our presence would be most welcome; and here we are. Someone with influence must have learned about our plans, because when we arrived, I had a plethora of jobs to choose from, and the planning for Paul's little business was waiting for his signature."

Andreas: "I'm not surprised by Paul's reception, but why were you so well treated?"

"You know, or maybe you don't, that I was a boarder at Newell Academy, just like Paul. My record there, and the school's recommendations, were every bit as good as his."

"I didn't know that. Thanks for the pocket history of New Bentwick. We love the place, too. We're even thinking of moving here."

"That's *brilliant!*"

The idea may have been brilliant, but this was the first I'd heard of it. What about my professional career?

Yet, after all, the people of New Bentwick might make fine grist for a behaviorist's mill. I began to feel what it truly was that I held.

9

The following Sunday it was Geoffrey's and Margot's turn to dine *chez nous*. Margot had already let me know that she would tell her story that evening, having first asked permission of Andreas, the other unblooded member of our group. I was surprised when she phoned me Saturday morning and asked if she could see me either that afternoon or the next: she had another story to tell me, one "for your ears only" that she urgently needed to confide to someone she trusted. I told her that we would be quite alone this afternoon—Andreas had a date to go fishing. Margot said she would walk over to our place around three-thirty.

There was only one possible path she could follow, so a little after three I set out in her direction. We met on the bridge over the little brook, we smiled and exchanged hugs, and began strolling arm in arm toward our house. Until now we'd signaled our sympathy for one another in ways limited by the circumstances of our weekly gatherings; this was the first time we were together just the two of us, and I'm certain Margot was as pleased by this as I was. We didn't talk much, perhaps no more than to name an end-of-season bird or flower; after which we'd walk on again in silence. This established between us a mode of judicious connivance; once we were settled on our west terrace over a pot of tea, Margot had no trouble in broaching her confidential subject.

"I feel I have to start by saying this: I'm a respectable person. The people who raised me—my father was a federal judge, my mother an exemplary nurse practitioner who tended her patients at all hours of the day and night—my grandparents, aunts, uncles, cousins, all likewise thoroughly respectable. And there wasn't a prude among them, and I'm no prude. What is it we all respect? Something like our vocations, or the ideas we have of ourselves. Respectful may be a better word for us. I worked diligently as a defender of women's rights, and you can't be a prude in that field and expect results—you wrangle daily about rape, abortion, intrauterine coils, bodily fluids, all the crass details of sexual life. As regards infidelity, I didn't have much of an opinion, it seemed more like a misdemeanor than a felony in the catalogue of sexual crime—I know it does a lot of damage, but I never saw why it *had* to. Myself, I'd never been tempted by it.

"You and Andreas know John of the notorious twins, don't you? So you've probably seen what fun he can be?"

"That's true—I've only been with him twice, but I thought he had a lot of charm, and sensitive, too—"

"Exactly! I'd only seen him twice myself, first at a semi-official drinks party Geoff took me to, I don't know why John was there—he walked all the way around a crowded room to introduce himself, which was flattering but also strange. The next time I sat next to him at a dinner at The Hunting Horn given by a bunch of town aldermen. He talked to me the whole evening through. It wasn't long before he began punctuating his pleasant conversation with remarks that became more and more affectionate. He didn't go so far as to declare his intentions, but when he told me how beautiful my eyes were, I recognized the seducer's most beguiling ploy. Still, he spoke the words ever so modestly, with his usual sweet smile, without a single blush or a drop of sweat on his smooth forehead. When we danced (slows only), he didn't dare place his cheek against mine but settled for the braided hair above it. As we said good night, he asked me if I'd have lunch with him in two days' time, meaning yesterday. I told him I'd have to check my dance card.

"He phoned yesterday morning. I'd told Geoff about the invitation; would he mind if I accepted? 'Why should I mind? John can't be after your favors. You must be near twenty years older than he is.'"

I interrupted: "Geoff doesn't know about the allure younger men find in older women? Why, operas have been written about it. When I met John, his inclination was all too plain. If much less explicit than in your case."

"I said nothing about that to Geoff. I agreed to the lunch.

"I'd come down on foot to meet him. He insisted on walking me home, and I let him. He followed me into the house, and once inside, he frankly defined his passion. He defined it with great delicacy and simplicity, and as he spoke he began stroking my bare upper arms—it was his touch more than his words that won me over, it was like a woman's touch, a caress without weight or pressure, his fingertips barely grazing my skin. When he stroked my nipples through the silk of my dress, he touched them as if in passing, as if they were unfolding rosebuds he might come back to pluck. In bed the same fingers entranced my whole body, bit by bit, and when he came to *my* rosebud, ah, I shiver just thinking—he held it in his mouth until I was limp with glory; I gave up counting the times I came after I reached fifteen, no I'm kidding, but it's as though he wanted to make things last forever. He fucked me hard, too, twice. I'm still bewitched."

I said, "Darling, you hit the jackpot! Just looking at you brings me joy. A year ago I might have felt a slight soupçon of jealousy. But no more."

"I know—I guess I found myself a real mensch, and a randy one. And so cute!"

"Do you plan to go on seeing him?"

"I don't know. We made comforting noises to that effect. Nothing definite. What's your take on replays of unforgettable…"

"The pits."

"That bad?"

"Not objectively; but by comparison, that bad. What about Geoff?"

"He won't be a problem. I'll never tell him. I won't love him any less."

"Please don't!"

I went to the Hydes', with Andreas, the Sunday of that week. Andreas noticed that Margot looked exceptionally pretty. As for Geoffrey, who knows?

Margot began her scheduled story with apparent aplomb. "Our first story was the story of a man told by a woman. The second was the story of a man told by a man. Tonight, and none too soon, it will be the story of a woman told by a woman." Margot made this announcement with such bravado I apprehended a replay of her tryst with John. I needn't have worried.

"I met her when my parents brought me to England, when I was fifteen years old. Meredith was my age; we were classmates in the school I was sent to, both of us lonely souls happy to have found each other. We shared our pulp novels and our favorite singers—Randy Newman, Dionne Warwick (Meredith pronounced her name without the *w* in 'wick'). We dated local boys together—we were living in Hull for some reason, at the time a total dump. Meredith became involved with a thirty-year-old docker, a tall, blackhaired man, nice enough I thought, with an incredibly virile body—a hunk. His name was Shanks. In time he got her pregnant. When Meredith found the courage to tell her parents, they couldn't handle the news. One day they'd make her swear not to have an abortion, two days later they'd tell her not to worry, they'd arrange one for her. I remember there being talk about a kind gynecologist in Geneva. In the end, however, he wasn't needed. Mr. Shanks stepped up and offered to marry 'his lassie.' Five months later their son was born and baptized a proper Anglican.

"So far so good. Shanks treated Meredith with a tenderness I hadn't expected, all through her pregnancy and during the sometimes difficult times afterwards. He treated the boy less warmly—I assumed that having been an orphan himself he'd never experienced the comforts of family affection and wouldn't know how to reinvent them now. That turned out to be too kind a view. Shanks's attitude gradually turned into open resentment, as if his generosity and affection in marrying Meredith had provoked a slow backlash of brutality. He used to curse his son or yell at him when he'd done nothing to warrant this abuse—when he'd done nothing at all. Apparently Shanks loathed the boy for simply existing.

"Meredith couldn't find any way to counter such unreason. Her only recourse was to keep the little boy out of Shanks's sight, something she did ever more frequently after the father moved on from verbal to physical chastisement. He started slapping and spanking him when he was three. At four Shanks used a cane, a hairbrush, or a strap. I begged Meredith to find a counselor or a specialist to attend to Shanks, or convince a doctor to prescribe some sedative she could dope him with, but she kept taking the blame for what was happening, and *he* started threatening *her* with violence if she tried to get medical or legal help. But when her son was six years old, and Shanks took a small board to him, and ended up breaking his hip ... I finally came to my senses. I couldn't take any more of it."

Andreas looked at me incredulously. Why wasn't I more surprised? I wasn't at all. Geoffrey, crouching by her chair, kissing her hand: "Why didn't you warn me that you were going to tell them?" Margot: "I'm all right. Of course—it's *my* story. I've very much wanted to tell it ever since Geoff came clean. Only I didn't want your sympathy to muddle the story line. It doesn't matter."

"Thank you, Margot, for telling it," I said.

She smiled at me: "Some things have to be told. Others, better not."

Andreas: "But then what happened?"

"What happened was that I took Timothy in the dead of

night and drove fifty miles to a trustworthy and highly reputed center that I'd had the brains to inquire about long
before that ghastly accident. We were at its gates when it
opened the next morning. By then I was at university where
I could call on a few eminences to vouch for me, and others
in the medical profession whom I'd consulted privately and
who were ready to certify the urgency of my predicament—I
was courteously received and attended to. I assented to the
formality of putting the boy up for adoption as the best way
to bypass bureaucratic delays (the institution was famous as
an adoption center, as well as an orphanage and school). I was
encouraged to take rooms nearby and spend my days with
Timothy while he became accommodated to his new life.

"The boy was a perfect angel through all of this—he sensed
that his new mentors were animated by kindness and concern,
and they in turn were touched by his sweetness, his openness,
no doubt his beauty, too! As long as all concerned were content with the arrangement, he could stay there as a boarder
until he finished his schooling. If I could pay one-third of his
tuition fees and as much for his board and lodging, the admin-
istrators of the center were reasonably sure they could obtain
the remainder in public and private scholarships.

"I spent a week visiting the buildings of this pleasant es-
tablishment in the company of Timothy and a certain Mr.
Ned Linnen, a teacher. He showed us the schoolrooms, the
refectory, several bedrooms, and the extensive playing fields.
Wherever we went, Timothy was introduced to students,
masters, and occasionally a guardian, most of whom greeted
him with benign curiosity. When I left him, I promised to
come back whenever he requested it. I kept my promise. As

the years passed, his requests came less and less frequently. I last saw him on his eleventh birthday.

"Soon after that I went back to Seattle, and while there, one year I went on a tour of the Far East during my summer vacation. I happened to visit New Bentwick, because a feminist companion told me there were 'interesting developments' going on there. I still don't know what she meant, but since I met Geoffrey almost as soon as I got off the boat, I didn't care, and a visit that was meant to last a few days—well, there's still no end in sight."

I asked her, "And Shanks?"

"The day after we left, I let him know by phone I wasn't coming back. He couldn't believe it. When I settled down in York, where I'd been studying, I wrote him a letter, in the manner of a case history of his life, as if written by a social investigator or a police officer. All cool, objective description. No judgments, no comments. It worked. He was mortified, wrecked. He still is. He begged me to see him. He's still doing it. I have a very happy life, except for one thing. He found out where I'd gone and followed me here. I've made sure he never gets near me. He lives alone, he survives doing menial jobs. I don't care. I don't want to hear about him."

Andreas: "How can you possibly be sure he won't bother you?"

"As soon as I learned he was here, I went to Father Murgatroyd, our Anglican priest. When I told him Shanks's history, he agreed to act as intermediary. An indictment, which has not been served, an indictment of Shanks for extreme child abuse, would, if activated, benefit from the testimony of the hospital staff and several dependable neighbors. Through

Father Murgatroyd, I conveyed to Mr. Shanks that if he ever approached me I would denounce him in this country, he would then be extradited to the UK for arrest and trial. He told the priest that he accepted my conditions, that he was content to stay here, out of my sight, in the hope that I might one day forgive him."

I said, "You're divorced?"

"I couldn't bring myself to do it. I'd kicked him out of my life. I'd taken his son away from him. He's living in penury. Divorce feels like one humiliation too many."

The telephone rang. Geoffrey, nearest to it, picked up. He turned back to us to announce the imminent arrival of Captain Kipper and Sergeant Kerr. "It seems something rather grisly has happened."

"Exit, pursued by a bear?"

"I'm afraid, Andreas, that they are not in a punning mood. Charley Kipper said that New Bentwick has at last recorded— a murder."

The two men soon appeared, haggard, and of somber mien. Margot said, "You've not had dinner!" and disappeared toward the kitchen. After two double whiskies, rapidly dispatched, bowls of hot broth were set before the new guests, soon followed by plates of cold meat and a bottle of red wine. They addressed their dinner with little relish. A first few sips of wine helped them get started.

Captain Kipper: "What you're about to hear may be hard to stomach. Sergeant Kerr, please tell our friends what you first witnessed."

"Certainly, sir. I remember the whole beginning—it was a seesaw of the right throbs and the wrong. I was strolling along the shore on a routine patrol, just past the town on the north side. It was pleasant walking at that hour, a lovely late afternoon with a quiet sea to my left and to my right a familiar countryside bathed in the mild light of Indian summer. Around five o'clock, just when the first shadows from the hills were darkening the waterfront, I saw at a distance two men coming towards me. I was able to identify Paul, one of the twins you're all so interested in."

Captain Kipper: "You're sure it was Paul, Sergeant?"

"It was the way he was manhandling his companion, almost dragging him along. I couldn't see John doing that. But Paul—you remember when we had to bring him in and scare him a little for taking his fists to one of his Arab workers?

"It took me a while to place the other man. He was an older fellow in his fifties, a poor sad bloke who goes by the name of Shanks—by his family name, strange as that may seem. Mr. Shanks kept shrinking from Paul the twin, who was holding him fast by his right arm and waving something at his head that I apprehended might be a pistol, and that indeed it was, as I clearly saw when they had drawn closer. I then turned round and without actually running I hastened as fast as I might—"

Charley Kipper intervened: "You may not know this, our men never carry firearms on their daily patrols. They are under strictest orders never to challenge an armed suspect whatever the circumstances. If Sergeant Kerr had intervened at any moment during the events that followed, he would have probably been deprived of his rank."

Alastair Kerr: "I knew the rule, and I also had not the slightest wish to be shot at! I kept hurrying towards Paul's boat, where I assumed he was going. It was tied up to a kind of shed set back from the water. I had time to get to its far side and clamber into the shed's underpinning, an assemblage of posts and struts meant to keep it above high water. I was well ensconced when I heard the men climbing onto the planks overhead.

"As soon as they were inside Shanks began protesting loudly. Then came a short, dull sound, after which he fell silent, at least he uttered no more words, only gulps or groans. I guessed that Paul had inserted a gag of some kind into Shanks's mouth, an onion as we found out, secured with heavy-duty tape across the lips and right around his head. He must before that have been attached to a seat of some sort. Paul then initiated his own tirade of insults. He began, 'Am I so changed, Old Fart, that you do not know your son?' in clear tones, but after that in a mumbled voice, so that I could not recognize every word, but the gist was Paul vehemently rebuking Shanks for pain and shame inflicted in some former time, with beatings never deserved, and accompanying this there was an irregular rumble of grunts due to the jabs Shanks was getting, kicks, too, judging from the sounds. I dared not use my mobile phone since he would surely hear me, as he would if I tried to climb out of my coop of old boards.

"There was a pause of almost a minute, then Paul started speaking again, now in a louder voice—I could catch all his words. 'Say, dear father, do you see this board? Remember? It's the one you busted my hip with, in memory of which I have cherished it through the years. I've kept it for you, just for you, right now.'"

(Only then did I let myself steal a look at Margot. She had turned her back to us.)

"I heard a loud smack, then Paul's voice. 'And now, Daddy-o, you are to take leave of this valley of perpetual dreams. Slowly, though. So best I help you get started. Just keep your eye on the board.' Several blows made a new crunching noise. When we examined the corpse, we deduced that Paul had struck Shanks with the edge of the board until the bridge of the nose and the neighboring sockets were crushed. Shanks's bleats were hard to bear. I felt myself doubtful again, felt indeed sure I was making a mistake. But I remembered the rule and Paul's gun, a large automatic pistol, the kind that could take a Maori's arm off. The bleating ended when Paul started bashing the skull. Shanks quickly lost consciousness, but it took considerable time to sunder the cranial bones."

Captain Kipper again broke in. "Thank you, Mr. Kerr. Let me tell the rest." Poor Kerr was visibly relieved; he had turned white with nausea.

"The Sergeant clambered out of his hiding place as soon as Paul's boat, with Shanks dragged aboard, had started down the ways. It disappeared northwards, its motor idle, on the current known as the Hawing Drift. Sergeant Kerr alerted our headquarters at once on his portable phone, then ran all the way there to give us a summary report. I ordered a pickup van carrying six men and one of our little patrol boats to join us in covering the shoreline north of Paul's shed. We dropped two men at the shed with orders to cordon it off with police tape and guard it until they were relieved."

Andreas broke in: "Captain Kipper, what is the Hawing Drift?"

"It's a current that's active only at this time of year. It rises off the bottom of our main street and follows the shoreline north at a distance of about twenty yards until it reaches an insignificant prong of land called The Chicken's Beak. There it makes a grand swing of 110 degrees to the southeast and maintains that direction as far as The Droppings, a pile of giant submarine blocks in the middle of the bay, and there it disappears. No one has been able to explain the course of the Drift or even how it came to exist." Andreas nodded his acknowledgment.

"We found Shanks off The Chicken Beak in about ten feet of water. He'd had two bricks sewn into his belly to keep him under water, but the job was bungled, the seams hadn't held. Poor Z. Shanks! That's how he figured in our file." Sergeant Kerr: "What time shall we assign to his death?" "Seventeen hours forty-six minutes." The hour of sunset? I thought.

The Sergeant briefly took up the tale. "We found him floating twenty-some yards from the beach and brought him straight ashore."

The Captain continued, "Immersion in seawater had cleansed the remaining gristle of blood. Yet the top of his head was a pitiful ruin. The Sergeant took one look at it and tossed his cookies."

"That I did."

"Surely, Sergeant, you'd seen worse during the war—in Burma, if I'm not mistaken?"

"Oh, yes, sir, what with fragmentation shells, shrapnel, rifle grenades. But that was impersonal damage. This was deliberate—years of embottled fury being vented. He didn't do it with no old board, neither. Not to tear up skull bones. I did later manage to jimmy the onion out of his mouth. As big as a small grapefruit."

The Captain: "A number of bystanders had gathered on the strand to watch. Sergeant Kerr walked towards them and waved them back. He explained, 'Please leave us space to do our work. We're bringing a man ashore. The man is laid flat—he's bung.' I admonished the Sergeant, 'In plain English, please.' 'Forgive me, sir. I fear it's the situation'—meaning that for that one dramatic word, he'd slipped back into Australian lingo. Turning back to the crowd, he clearly cried, 'The min is did.' I then called Jerry to drive over with his beach van, and I bought them all ice creams.

"We then followed a hunch and kept to the Hawing Drift as it headed seawards. We spotted Paul's craft foundering on the eastern edge of The Droppings. Our boatman pulled alongside it and we secured it fore and aft to our longer vessel. Kerr and I then boarded Paul's boat.

"It was awash almost to the gunwales. There was nothing in the stern space but seagoing gear. Not much in the cabin. A low door in its forward bulkhead had been bolted shut on the far side, closing off the bow. The Sergeant found a large chisel and prised it open. The bow had sunk lower than the rest of the boat; the compartment beyond the door was flooded up to its roof. Sergeant Kerr crawled into it and quickly found Paul, who was completely submerged. He had tried weighing himself down with the light anchor and its chain—by whatever means, he'd succeeded in drowning. I helped the Sergeant drag him into the cabin and onto the deck, whence with a pair of ropes advanced by our boatman, we succeeded in transferring him to the patrol boat.

"There was next to nothing in his pockets—a few low-denomination bank notes, a pair of wire-rimmed reading glasses, two maroon bandanas, faded and now sodden—but Sergeant Kerr had found a small metal box in the cabin and brought it with him. We easily broke open its lock and in it found some informative documents—ones concerning his employers, two notes from his mother, educational certificates, including several from a place called Newell Academy. These prompted me, once I was back on land and at our headquarters, to put through a call to the said Academy.

"You may well ask, What? On a Sunday night? Well, thanks to the way the shifting time of the world has been sliced into zones, when it is eight in the evening here on Sunday, with every office in the land closed down, in bonny England it is (quite wonderfully, when you think about it) nine o'clock of a *Monday* morning with every soul in the land starting the working week! So I phoned Newell Academy. It was buzzing with wakefulness. I was switched to a lady in the department of records—a Mrs. Banyard—who sounded thrilled when I asked her to find information about one of their former wards. I was sure only of his surname as it appeared in the documents—Shanks, to be sure. I suggested Paul as his given name, but there had been no such person. Still I knew that it *was* Paul because in his school pictures he was perfectly recognizable (at least as one of the twins), something not at all the case in the photographs affixed to his last job applications."

Margot had grown more and more agitated throughout the policemen's account. At the mention of Newell Academy she started sobbing. She now said, in a weepy bark, "The given name is Timothy." Long before this Geoffrey had moved her to a comfortable settee, where she now sat between him and me in cruel distress that sharpened no matter what we said to her or how tenderly we held her.

The Captain told us that Mrs. Banyard had summarized all the information about Timothy Shanks in the Academy's files, including a detailed history of his long-suffering mother's role. She promised to send him the complete files overnight.

Geoffrey excused himself to step outside for "a breath of open air."

When he returned, Sergeant Kerr quietly suggested, "I think we all need a drink."

A coffee table appeared in our midst. On it were soon set a tray with six small tumblers, a carafe of cold water, and a bottle of Talisker. We mixed our own draughts.

After a while, in the silence that followed, Margot groaned, "What have I done?"

Geoffrey, again at her side, said to her, "My darling, I'm sick with shame. I still don't understand." Into her nearer ear I softly growled, "He must *never* know!"

Another long silence was broken when one of Margot's earrings fell to the floor. The proverbial pin. I felt a tear congeal under my left eye; it was at that moment that I noticed the lambent gleam emanating from the Sergeant's pate.

"Margot—Mrs. Shanks—" Captain Kipper began, "I'm not sure how to address you. My question is essentially an official one. If Timothy Shanks is Paul, what was John's given name?"

"John?"

"His twin. He's disappeared—without a trace, as one says. I found Wicheria, even she hasn't a clue as to his whereabouts."

"His twin? Charley, you spoke to this woman at the school.

She told you all about me. You know I never had but one child—my darling Timmy."

Geoffrey must have forgotten to close the front door after his breath of air; it now slammed shut. Beyond it a warm north wind was rising, reminding us that as April ends, autumn begins: a time of mists and moister winds, and a few chilly snaps; of local wines, cooled a long age; of early nights by electric light; inventing names, and guessing games; and your soft laugh.

KEY WEST, MAY 15, 2015
PARIS, AUGUST 1, 2016